DESTINY AT DRY CAMP

DESTINY AT DRY CAMP

JOHN D. NESBITT

FIVE STAR
A part of Gale, Cengage Learning

GALE
CENGAGE Learning·

Farmington Hills, Mich • San Francisco • New York • Waterville, Maine
Meriden, Conn • Mason, Ohio • Chicago

GALE
CENGAGE Learning®

LIBRARY OF CONGRESS CATALOGING-IN-PUBLICATION DATA

Names: Nesbitt, John D., author.
Title: Destiny at Dry Camp / John D. Nesbitt.
Description: Waterville, Maine : Five Star Publishing, 2017.
Identifiers: LCCN 2016041922 (print) | LCCN 2016051415 (ebook) | ISBN 9781432834005 (hardcover) | ISBN 1432834002 (hardcover) | ISBN 9781432836887 (ebook) | ISBN 1432836889 (ebook) | ISBN 9781432833961 (ebook) | ISBN 1432833960 (ebook)
Subjects: LCSH: Ranchers—Fiction. | Murder—Investigation—Fiction. | BISAC: FICTION / Mystery & Detective / Historical. | FICTION / Westerns. | GSAFD: Western stories. | Mystery fiction.
Classification: LCC PS3564.E76 D47 2017 (print) | LCC PS3564.E76 (ebook) | DDC 813/.54—dc23
LC record available at https://lccn.loc.gov/2016041922

Find us on Facebook– https://www.facebook.com/FiveStarCengage
Visit our website– http://www.gale.cengage.com/fivestar/
Contact Five Star™ Publishing at FiveStar@cengage.com

Printed in Mexico
2 3 4 5 6 7 21 20 19 18 17

For Johnny D. Boggs, always the best.

CHAPTER ONE

The man named Dunbar came to our part of the country in the middle of the summer, when the rangeland was beginning to wither. Even a semi-arid region will have rain once in a while, sometimes in large doses that would do more good if they were portioned out, but any rainfall was welcome. When Dunbar arrived, the year I turned eighteen, we had had rainstorms and tornado-like weather in late May, but then the weather turned hot and dry. The grass had gone from a bright green to a darker, duller tone as the blades of grass grew thin.

Dunbar rode into the Harris Basin by way of the Clay Creek Ranch, where I was working at the time. I was out looking after cattle when I saw a rider appear, as if he had materialized out of the swells of grassland or had emerged from the hazy mountains well behind him to the north. I could see at a distance that he was a dark-featured man in a dark hat. He rode a blue roan and led a buckskin packhorse that carried his gear. He showed no intention of avoiding me but rather rode straight on to the knoll where I sat on my horse, waiting. The faint sound of hoofbeats carried on the still, dry air, and dust rose from the hooves of his two horses.

I had an awareness of being by myself in a vast sweep of country bordered by the Laramie Mountains on the east and north and by the main body of the Rocky Mountains on the west. As far as a person could see, not a tree was visible, nor ranch buildings or windmills. The sky above had a few hazy clouds, but the day was bright and warm.

The rider's horses moved toward me at a fast walk, picking up their feet. I heard their huffing breath, and then, as they came to a stop, the sounds settled with the rustle of leather.

The man sat straight in the saddle and raised a gloved hand in greeting. He was a good-sized man, taller than average, riding a horse that stood sixteen hands or a little more. He wore a high-crowned black hat, which matched his dark hair, dark eyes, and bushy mustache. He had broad, full shoulders and a high chest. I would have guessed him to be in his middle thirties, in his physical prime.

"Good afternoon," he said.

"How do you do?"

"Well enough." He smiled and let his eyes rove beyond me, to the south. "I assume this is the way to Dry Camp."

"That's right." I pointed with my thumb over my shoulder. "The town is about ten miles south of here. You can find it with no trouble."

He smiled again. "That's the way I like to find most places, with no trouble. But I'm not going there right away. What I'm looking for is the Clay Creek Ranch, which I understood was north of the town of Dry Camp."

"Well, it is, and you found it. I work for the Clay Creek Ranch, and they've got cattle out this way."

The man did not show surprise. He glanced at my horse and said, "I thought I might be close."

I pointed to the southwest. "About four miles that-a-way."

He nodded. "Thanks. Do you know if they're puttin' on any men?"

"I have no idea. Either the owner, Rich Stanton, or his foreman, Paul Kelso, would be in charge of that."

"And you are—?"

"Whit," I said. "Whit Barnett."

"Pleased to meet you. My name's Dunbar."

He turned his horse and leaned forward with his hand held out, so I moved my horse around to shake hands.

"Don't let me keep you from your work," he said.

"It's no trouble. But I suppose I should move along. Maybe I'll see you later."

"I hope so," he said. "That is, I hope they've got work for me."

"Of course. I wish you luck."

"And the same to you." He touched his hat brim and turned his horses in the direction where I had pointed.

I rode on in the opposite direction, keeping an eye out for cattle in the distance and gopher holes up close. I noted as before the drying grass, growing in bunches a hand's-width apart with patches of dirt showing in between. After a few minutes I looked in back of me, in time to see Dunbar and his two horses disappearing into the landscape.

Shadows were stretching out from the buildings as I rode into the ranch yard. Dunbar's two horses were tied to a hitching rail in the shade of the barn, while Dunbar himself sat on a wooden crate and leaned against the door post. The horses perked up their ears and turned their heads as my horse clip-clopped on the hard ground. Dunbar stood up and walked forward.

"Have you talked to anyone?" I asked.

"Not yet. Not about hiring, anyway. I spoke with the cook, and he said either the boss or the foreman should be along soon. Does the boss ride out like the rest of the men?"

"He lives in town, but sometimes he stays here. That's his house. He comes and goes, so he doesn't ride out on a regular basis. Which means, I guess, that he doesn't come in on a regular basis, either. I hope you don't have to wait too long."

Dunbar flexed his arms as he pushed out his chest and took

in a breath. "No hurry. Just get a little drowsy, sittin' in one place."

I swung down from my horse and loosened the cinch. My horse gave a shake, rattling the buckles and leather and bits. When the noise subsided, I heard the footfalls of a horse behind me.

I turned and saw the boss, Rich Stanton, riding in on a red dun. The horse walked at a slow pace, and Rich had an unhurried air about him. I wondered which direction he had come from, because if he had been on the trail behind me, he wouldn't have ridden in so soon at that pace.

He dismounted and walked forward a few steps. He carried himself with authority, which I was used to seeing, but I wondered how a man like Dunbar took him. Stanton was older, between forty-five and fifty, with blond hair that was paling with middle age. He wore a high-crowned, cream-colored hat with four dents in the peak so that it looked like a pyramid with a rounded tip. He was dressed as usual, in a neat suit of light tan set off in contrast by his dark brown gunbelt. He wore light-colored gloves of the kind called doeskin, but I could not say with certainty what they were made of.

After a nod in my direction, he turned his attention toward Dunbar. "Good afternoon," he said. "Some way I can help you?"

"Wondering if there's any work to be had."

"Name?"

"J.R. Dunbar, sir."

"Rich Stanton."

The men shook—one light, one dark, both wearing gloves. Stanton said, "I take it you know how to ride." He tossed a glance at Dunbar's roan and buckskin.

"I can keep from falling off a gentle horse."

"And rope?"

"Head 'em, heel 'em, or trip 'em. Not to brag, but I can hold my own."

Stanton's eyes did not stay on Dunbar for long. He glanced again at Dunbar's horses and stared out at the range. "Not much need of help right now," he said.

Dunbar nodded.

"But I'll need a good hand later, for fall roundup." Stanton's eyes flickered at Dunbar and moved away. "I'll tell you what. If you want to stay on at a dollar a day, I can try you out. If I decide I want to keep you on, we'll talk again about wages for roundup."

"Sounds all right."

"Should be." Stanton's eyes came back to Dunbar. "Where are you from?"

"I come from the North."

"The North. As in North versus South?"

"Just the North," said Dunbar. "The land of the pale blue snow."

Stanton laughed. "It gets damn cold here, too, though you wouldn't know it at this time of year."

"Seems that way. But after a while in any cold country, a man can remember it on the sunniest day of the year."

"Isn't that the truth," said Stanton. Again his eyes did not rest long on the stranger. "You can put your horses in the corral, and my foreman, Kelso, will tell you which ones to ride. He'll give you your daily orders, too."

"Much obliged," said Dunbar.

"A pleasure." Stanton handed me the reins of the red dun. "Take care of this." With a nod to each of us hired hands, he walked away in the direction of his ranch house.

I put away the two ranch horses, the boss's red dun and the sorrel I was riding, as Dunbar unsaddled the roan and unloaded the buckskin. When he was finished, the two of us walked across

11

the ranch yard to the bunkhouse. A light, dry breeze floated in from the northwest, and the *chuck-chuck* of a blackbird carried from an elm tree on the west side of the yard.

"How long have you worked here?" Dunbar asked.

"Just a couple of months. Since May. I started at the lowest level, and I haven't moved up much."

"Everyone's got to start somewhere," he said. "It seems like no matter where you go, things could go lower. You just don't realize it until the situation comes around. And on the higher end—well, there's always someone who's got more authority, once you get out of your own little world."

"That's a good thing to remember," I said. "Sometimes I forget about the larger world out there. Here, you don't have to look very far to see the top dog. And like I've said, I can look at my own feet and see the bottom."

Dunbar laughed. "With no reference to this place, of course, your top dog is on top only in a dog's world. And out in the larger world, as you call it, even the greatest men have to meet their maker." After a couple of steps in silence, he added, "You strike me as someone who likes to think for himself."

"I haven't formed my own philosophy of life, but I like to think about what I've learned. This kind of work gives a person time for that."

Dunbar had a droll expression on his face as he said, "Isn't that the truth."

I smiled. I was pretty sure I heard an echo.

Hamp, the bunkhouse cook, had a sullen look on his meaty face, and his overgrown yellow hair lay like a mat over his temples. He paid little attention to Dunbar as he assigned him a bunk, then turned his back on both of us and resumed cutting up spuds. I had gathered that Hamp did not like newcomers, and as I was still more or less in that category, I was used to being ignored.

Dunbar looked at me and said, "How many men bunk here?"

Hamp turned around. "Six, with you," he said.

Hamp had his own cot in a kind of a boar's nest in the cook shack half of the building, apart from the hired men's bunks. As I ran a quick tally, I saw that he did not include himself in the count.

"Thanks," said Dunbar. "Just curious, is all."

"I've got to know how many I cook for, even though they always send me more on short notice."

Dunbar nodded. I was glad he didn't answer. I had learned that the sooner a fellow let Hamp have the last word, the better.

I hung my hat and stretched out on my bunk. Dunbar sat on the edge of his. After a few minutes, the room brightened as the door opened. Slater and Blythe, who rode out and came in together even when they worked apart, walked in with a jingle of spurs and hung their hats on pegs. I sat up and introduced them to Dunbar.

"Welcome to the ranch," said Slater. "I hope you get along well with everyone."

"Thanks," said Dunbar. "I usually make out all right."

Blythe said, "Take off your hat. Make yourself at home."

"I will. But I need to fetch my bag and bedroll first."

I swung around and sat up. "I'll go with you."

"I can carry it all myself."

"I'll go."

"As you wish."

We both stood up and headed for the door. Dunbar paused as I retrieved my hat, and in that instant, the door opened again. Half in shadow with the evening sun behind him, Paul Kelso stood in the doorway.

"Huh," he said. "You must be the new man. Boss mentioned you."

"I'm new here."

Kelso looked him up and down. "I'm the foreman, Paul Kelso."

"Pleased to meet you. My name's Dunbar."

After they shook hands, Kelso did not move from the doorway. He was not a big man, being of middle height and middle build, but he struck an obstinate pose with his head tipped back. He wore a short-brimmed, light-brown hat with a crown that narrowed to a point in front. He had straight blond hair and a flushed complexion, with a rounded area above his upper lip, so that his lip tightened over his upper teeth when he talked. "Are you goin' somewhere?" he asked.

"I'm goin' to bring in my blankets and warbag."

Kelso lingered. He wore an ivory-handled .45 in a tooled holster that rode down on his hip, and he had a habit of dangling his hand as if he was ready to draw. "Sure," he said. "Don't let me keep you." He hung his thumb on his belt and stepped aside. "You goin', too, kid?"

"Thought I would," I said.

The corners of his mouth tucked back, and his upper lip tightened. "Helper," he said. He nodded as he gave Dunbar another looking over. "Won't be long till suppertime."

Dunbar did not answer, but as he began to move toward the door, Kelso spoke again.

"A man's allowed to have two horses of his own here. But when you're workin', you ride ranch horses. Just thought I'd mention it."

"You bet. Sounds reasonable to me."

On the way to the barn, I felt as if I should apologize for Hamp and Kelso, but I couldn't think of a way to make it sound right. So I held my tongue, and I assumed Dunbar could see for himself that not everyone at the Clay Creek Ranch was of the same mind.

Dunbar let me shoulder his bedroll as he carried his warbag with one hand and his rifle and scabbard with another. Dusk was falling, and the leaves of the elm tree whispered in the breeze. Halfway across the ranch yard, Dunbar said, "Sounds like a horse."

I stopped and heard hoofbeats coming in at a fast walk. "That'll be Willard," I said.

"The sixth man."

"That's right. He'll be in before long."

Hamp was setting a platter of fried potatoes on the table when we walked into the bunkhouse. A haze of tobacco smoke hung in the lamplight and mixed with the smoke and vapors from the kitchen. The smell of fried meat lifted my spirits.

Slater, Blythe, and Kelso sat along one side of the table, so Dunbar and I took chairs on the other side. Kelso stubbed out a cigarette in a sardine can and rolled a glance at Dunbar, but he said nothing.

"Pass this along and serve yourselves," said Hamp. "The meat will be ready in a couple of minutes."

The serving spoon clacked on the crockery platter as the potatoes went down the other side of the table. Hamp brought out a plate of fried beef and started it down the same way. All five of us had served ourselves and had begun to eat when the bunkhouse door opened and Willard walked in.

He hung his hat on a peg, swirled his hands in the wash basin, and wiped them on his shirt. He sat down at the remaining place on our side of the table and began serving himself some potatoes and meat. I was used to seeing Willard, and he seemed normal to me, but as I saw him now as if through Dunbar's eyes, I realized he had much darker skin than anyone else at the table. He kept to himself, not looking long at anyone and not talking.

Kelso spoke up. "You almost missed supper, Willard. What

happened? Did you fall asleep?"

Willard's dark eyes flashed, and his white teeth showed as he spoke. "I had a long ride."

"You ought to be like the kid here. First one back. He's not gonna get lost in the dark."

"Neither am I."

"You'd better not. Because if we had to go out lookin' for you, we might have a hard time findin' you. Fella back home, he always had a horse with white socks so he could find him in the dark."

Willard ignored Kelso's remark and looked past me on our side of the table. He had a narrow nose, straight black hair, and high cheekbones. He did not look Negro, Mexican, or Indian to me, and I wondered how Dunbar perceived him. In a civil tone, Willard said, "Are you a new hand, or just stayin' the night?"

"I just got hired," said Dunbar.

Willard drew his mouth together. "I seen your two horses in the corral and your packsaddle in the barn."

"My name's Dunbar."

"Mine's Willard, which I guess you already heard." He took a bite of meat. "Anyway, good to meet you."

"Likewise."

Hamp set a bowl of boiled rice and raisins on the table. "Here's speckled puppy, for them that wants dessert."

Kelso said, "Back home, they serve it with cream."

"Well, we've got no milk cow here, and I don't know who'd milk it if we had one."

"I've pulled on a few titties," said Kelso. "How about you, Willard?"

"Don't know a thing about it."

Hamp ignored Willard and spoke to Kelso. "I doubt you'd milk one now."

Kelso had his hand resting on the table with his knife sticking straight up. "You're right about that. It's women's work. Women and kids and old men with no teeth left in their mouth. Some of those girls back home, now, they could milk a cow."

"Well, if you get one here, let me know. But I think it'll be a long wait."

"Maybe some day I'll surprise you."

"That's one way you could do it."

Slater spoke up. "I'll have some of that rice pudding."

I was glad he spoke when he did. Kelso and Hamp might have gone on for a while, seeing who could get in the last word.

For breakfast, Hamp served fried bacon and a cold cornmeal mush that he carved out of the pot in slabs. "Eat up," he said. "This'll stick to your ribs."

Kelso said, "Back home, they eat this mush when it's hot."

"I know. And they serve it with cream."

Kelso turned to me and said, "Whit, I'm gonna have you and the new man clean corrals today. You know where the tools are."

"Yep." I glanced at Dunbar, and I was sure it was obvious to him as well that Kelso was trying him out.

Kelso turned to Blythe and Slater. "You boys can take the ride over east." He tightened the corners of his mouth. "Willard, you can circle over west. Don't get lost." He took a breath. "Nothin' new for anyone. We can all come back for noon dinner."

Blythe said, "Did Rich go back to town last night?"

"I believe he did. Do you put bacon grease in the mush, Hamp?"

"Not for people. That's for coonhounds."

"Just checkin'." Kelso looked around the table as he took hold of the platter of bacon. "Well, everyone knows what they're gonna do today."

★ ★ ★ ★ ★

The sun warmed things up right away in the corrals. Dunbar did not show any dislike for the work, although he had to mop away the sweat each time he lifted the black hat for ventilation. When we took a few minutes to stand in the shade at midmorning, he set his hat back on his head and smoothed his bushy mustache with his gloved hand.

"What's the problem with Kelso?" he asked.

"In what way?"

"He seems to have it in for Willard."

"That's the way he is. He doesn't like Negroes, Mexicans, Indians, or any foreigners. Not just Chinese, but Bohemians and even Swedes. He's got low words for all of them."

"I can imagine. He sounds like he's from the South, but I can't always pick out the separate accent."

"He's from Texas. You'll hear him say things like 'Remember the Alamo' and 'The South will rise again.' "

"Then I'd guess those girls back home aren't German milk-maids."

I laughed. "I'm sure they speak English."

"How is he with cattle?"

"He came up with the Texas herds, so he knows something. But the boss decides how to manage the ranch."

"I can see that. And besides, this whole business is different than it was when the first herds came. Fences, windmills, hay meadows. You don't just turn your cows out for the winter and take a count in the spring." Dunbar smiled. "These fellas who used to say they wouldn't do any work except on horseback, a lot of 'em have calluses from pitchin' hay and mendin' ditch-banks." He gave an amused expression. "My kind of girl, and I'd guess yours, too, doesn't mind the texture of a working man's hands."

I said, "Growing up in Ohio, some of us picked berries for

our money. I knew boys who didn't want the girls to see the stains on their hands. But as one farmer told me, don't ever be ashamed to let people know you work."

"Well said. I don't know if all work is good work, but there's such a thing as honest work, and there's no reason to be afraid of it. Or ashamed. Our foreman might be pleased to stick us on a job he would hate, but it doesn't bother me a bit." He pushed out his lips, and his mustache moved. "Well, it *is* manure. Not quite as pleasant as a crate of strawberries."

"Blackberries. But they do grow strawberries in Ohio. Quite a few."

"I thought they did."

Slater and Blythe rode into the yard at noontime while Kelso was looking over the work that Dunbar and I had done. They stopped where the three of us stood.

"What's up?" said Kelso.

Slater answered. "I guess Carlyle needs a little help."

"Doin' what?"

"That old man, Guilford, that works for him, got lost. Carlyle would like some help findin' him."

"How many does he need?"

"The bunch of us, if he can get us to help. Said the old man's been missin' since yesterday afternoon."

Kelso looked all around the ranch yard and gave out a huff of breath. "I suppose so. Some old man working for a dirt farmer wanders off, and we've all got to drop what we're doing."

"It could happen to anyone," Slater said.

"Yeah. Like Willard. Well, let's eat, and not waste any time."

Kelso pointed out a sorrel horse and told Dunbar to ride it. He assigned me a stocky bay. Slater, Blythe, and Willard picked out horses from their strings, as did Kelso. In less than fifteen minutes, the six of us were saddled up and riding out.

Dunbar and I rode a ways back, so as not to eat so much dust. When we were under way, Dunbar asked what I knew about the old man who was missing.

An image of Ross Guilford had come to my mind several times in the last hour, and it appeared again in the form of a white-haired, pale-complexioned old man with fragile skin that had broken veins. He had a thin nose, washed-out blue eyes, and a week's white stubble. I recalled the old, dusty black hat with a rolled brim and a creased crown, plus old black boots broken out in the toes. He was lean and bent over, and he walked slow.

"He's an old man," I said. "An old stove-up cowpuncher who does a little work for Tom Carlyle. He looks after Tom's cattle and earns his keep that way."

"Is he likely to get lost?"

"You wouldn't think so. But he's close to the end of his days, I think, and he might have had to get off his horse somewhere and can't pull himself back on. Something like that." In truth, I pictured him lying on his back, eyes wide to the sky, as ants traveled over his chest. It was a normal thought, given what the old man had looked like the few times I saw him.

"Let's hope we find him. Even if he's looking at the end, some ways are better than others. How far is it to Carlyle's?"

"About ten miles west. I don't think we'll have to go that far, from what Slater and Blythe said."

We rode west for about an hour and stopped for a rest. Kelso squatted in the shade of his horse, rolled a cigarette, and lit it. Dunbar watched as the man poked the dead match under the toe of his boot and mashed it into the dirt.

"We'll fan out here," said Kelso. "If you find something, fire a shot in the air. Count off a minute, and fire again. That'll help the rest of us locate you."

Dunbar watched as the other three rolled cigarettes and lit them. Willard paced back and forth as he smoked. Kelso gave a slow, upward turn of his head.

"Why don't you settle down, Willard?"

"There's an old man out here somewhere."

Kelso spit a fleck of tobacco. "Chances are, he's beyond our help. But if you can't stand still, why don't you get goin'?"

Willard tossed down his half-smoked cigarette and stepped on it. "I will. I'll go north about a mile and turn west." He stepped up into the saddle, light and quick, and took off.

Dunbar said, "We can go next if you want."

"Sure," said Kelso. "You and then the kid. Stay about a quarter of a mile apart."

Off we rode. The rangeland was very similar to the area where I had ridden the day before. Dirt showed through the sparse grass. The sagebrush grew close to the ground, no higher than two inches. The sky was hazy under the bright sun. I did not see any buzzards, but that did not mean anything. I had come upon dead cows, ripe and bloating, with no buzzards in view for miles around. Magpies and coyotes, on the other hand, seemed always to be close by, and they did not miss much. I kept an eye out for them, not only in front of me but on either side, where one of the other riders might scare up something.

The heat of the afternoon set in, and a drowsiness settled on me as the bay horse plugged along. Nothing moved on the grassland—not so much as a prairie dog or a jackrabbit. My head bobbed, and I had to lift my head and widen my eyes. I imagined German milkmaids, Gypsy girls with tambourines, Mexican señoritas with gourds of water in the arbors of adobe haciendas.

A shot brought me wide awake. I stopped the horse and listened. A minute later, another shot sounded. I placed it to the south, and I thought I heard a voice. I turned the bay horse, spurred him into a trot, and spurred him again so that he hit a lope. The ground flowed beneath me as I kept an eye out for gopher holes. In spite of his bulk, the bay had a smooth lope and ate up the ground. After several minutes, I topped a rise and slowed the horse to a walk. Less than half a mile to the southeast, three men stood in front of their horses looking at the ground. I recognized them as Slater, Blythe, and Kelso. I kept the bay at a walk, and within a couple of minutes I heard a horse coming up behind me. I shifted in the saddle and saw Dunbar on his way to join me. As the sorrel horse came to a jolting, heaving slowdown, Dunbar spoke.

"Looks like they found something."

Closer, I caught my first glimpse of the body, lying in one of the hundred poses I had imagined. Ross Guilford lay on his stomach, head turned, one arm tucked beneath him and the other stretched out beyond his head. His white hair reflected the sunlight, while his dark hat lay a few feet away.

Dunbar and I came to a stop and dismounted. With the reins in his hand, Dunbar crouched by the body.

"It's all over for him." Dunbar pushed at the bent elbow. "Pretty stiff. I'd say he's been here a while."

Footfalls from another horse caused everyone to look around. Tom Carlyle rode toward us at a walk. He was wearing a brown hat that cast his face in shadow, and he was dressed like a farmer with suspenders and a shirt with rolled-up sleeves. He wore clodhopper boots that stuck through the large wooden stirrups on his saddle.

"That's what I was afraid of," he said. "I found his horse off by itself with the reins trailing. Just poking along and eating grass."

"Looks like he fell from his horse," Kelso said.

Carlyle shook his head. "I don't know. That horse he rides is dog-gentle."

Dunbar, still kneeling, said, "He appears to have been injured in the back of the head."

"It happens," said Kelso. "Depends on how they fall off."

Dunbar stood up. "When a man gets thrown, he usually has dirt on him. Sometimes quite a bit."

Carlyle's eyes had narrowed. "It doesn't make any sense. He might have been old, but he was natural on a horse. I can't imagine that horse throwin' him, but I've got no idea of why someone would want to do him in. He was an honest old man, trying to live out his days the best way he knew how."

Kelso cleared his throat. "Well, I'm sorry for him, and I'm sorry for you, Tom. What do you think we should do?"

Carlyle sniffled. "I don't know. I guess we can take him back to my place."

Kelso waved at Slater and Blythe. "These two boys can help you. The rest of us will head back. If you need somethin', be sure to let us know."

Time seemed to stand still. I had a faint ringing in my ears, and I had no awareness of anyone doing anything.

Kelso's voice brought me out of my daze. "Let's go, kid."

Things came back into motion. Blythe and Slater were leaning over the body. Carlyle was climbing down from his horse. Dunbar was mounting up and turning the sorrel away. Still, everything seemed wrong, and no one seemed to be setting things right.

Kelso said, "Come on."

I did not recall having gotten off my horse, but I had to climb back on. I did so, and I was about to rein my horse around when a rumble of hoofbeats sounded. Willard came drumming down the slope and brought his horse to a stop in front of our group. His eyes were open wide.

Kelso said, "We're ready to go, Willard. They found the old

man, and these other boys are going to take care of him."

Willard swung down slow from his horse. "I'll be along."

"I said, let's go."

"And I said, I'll be along."

"Suit yourself," said Kelso. "But we've done as much good here as we can do."

He slapped his reins and led the way. Dunbar and I followed, leaving the rest of the group out in the middle of the vast rangeland.

CHAPTER TWO

Kelso sat by himself at the table in the bunkhouse, smoking a cigarette, as Hamp banged around in the kitchen getting supper ready. Slater and Blythe had come back from Carlyle's and were stretched out on their bunks, while Dunbar and I sat up on ours. Dunbar caught a glance at Kelso now and then, but the foreman paid no attention. He sat aloof in a haze of smoke. I was used to seeing him in a poor humor, even sulky, but something was different now. I realized it was his silence. I had not known him to go so long without talking.

Supper came to the table, and Willard had not shown up yet. Each man served himself a bowl of beans and took a biscuit from the tin plate. One biscuit was left over.

No one spoke. The meal progressed with a clatter of spoons against the crockery dishes. A second plate of biscuits was moving down the table when the bunkhouse door opened and Willard walked in.

Kelso ignored him and said, "Hamp cooks a good pot of beans. He puts in plenty of rind, and he doesn't scrimp with the ham."

The cook had taken a seat at the end of the table near the kitchen. He raised his head and gave a slight nod in acknowledgment.

"Good biscuits," said Blythe.

"Best when they're hot." Kelso tossed a glance at the lone biscuit in front of Willard's place at the table.

Willard served himself a bowl of beans and sat down. He did not look at anyone or say anything.

Kelso said, "You seem to be moping more than usual, Willard."

"A man died."

"We know that."

"He was someone I'd known my whole life."

Kelso's upper lip stretched over his teeth. "He'd seen a lot of years. Everyone's got to go when his time comes, and the old man would be the first to tell you. And he wouldn't want people mopin' about it."

"That's easy for you to say."

"I've seen men younger than you go to their deaths. Horse fallin' over backwards, steam engine blowin' up. They wouldn't have wanted any snivelin', either."

Willard broke his cold biscuit and dipped half of it in his beans.

Kelso didn't let up. "Sometimes I wonder how you come to be a moper. I wonder if it's in your blood."

Willard did not answer.

"Is it?"

Willard still did not say anything.

"You sit with your muddy moping face and don't answer."

"I've already said enough."

Dunbar shifted in his chair. He was sitting on my right, and Willard sat on my left. Kelso sat across from Dunbar, so he spoke diagonally across the table.

"Maybe it's just as well." Kelso scooted his chair backward, stood up, and carried his bowl and spoon to the dishpan. When he sat down again, he took out his jackknife and began cleaning his fingernails.

The rest of us continued with our meal. It was not unusual for Kelso to finish first, as he was not a heavy eater, and he did not worry about cleaning his fingernails or smoking a cigarette while the rest of us were still eating. So I paid him no mind until I heard the knife click shut.

His chair scraped as he stood up. I saw that he did not slip his knife into his pocket but closed over it with his fist. He took slow steps behind Blythe and Slater and around the end of the table where Hamp sat, until he came to a stop at Willard's left.

Dunbar took in a deep breath and turned in his chair. I set my spoon down. Slater and Blythe had paused and were watching as well.

Kelso's voice was steady as he said, "Look up at me when I talk to you, Willard. I've got somethin' to say."

Willard tipped his head.

"I'll tell you, I didn't like the way you talked back to me this afternoon. When I say let's go, that's what we do."

I could not see Willard's face, but Kelso's was tight and more flushed than usual.

"I don't take that sort of thing from any man that's under me, you know? Maybe you've got it in your mulatto blood to be stubborn, but you don't do that with me."

Willard's voice was calmer than I would have expected. "I'm not a mulatto."

"I don't know what else you are. Your mother was."

My heartbeat picked up, and I heard Dunbar's chair squeak.

Willard said, "She was a Creole. You didn't know her."

Kelso's lip was stretched tight. "You're right that I never seen her, but all them Creoles got colored blood in 'em."

Dunbar spoke up. "I think you ought to let it go."

Hamp was looking at Dunbar as if for the first time. Slater and Blythe had their eyes wide open. My heart was in my throat, as I was seated with Dunbar at my shoulder and Kelso glaring past me.

Kelso's face had turned a deeper red, and his neck was

strained. He said, "For a fella that just rode in on the grubline, you've got a little too much to say about things that are none of your business."

Dunbar stood up and away from the table. He said, "When you put things in terms like you did, I make it my business."

"What terms?"

"Color."

Kelso gave Dunbar a hard stare, and standing straight up with his shoulders back, he took four slow steps around Willard and past me. With his hands low at his sides, he loosened his shoulders and said, "Well, let me tell you somethin' about how things—"

His right hand came up and around, with the folded knife held tight as if it was a brass bar. Dunbar's left hand shot up to block it, and his right fist landed on Kelso's cheekbone. Kelso's head jerked back, and his feet went out from under him.

Chairs scraped and thumped as everyone stood up to get out of the way. Dunbar stood with his fists ready, while Kelso lay propped up on his elbow, feeling the side of his head.

"See here," said Hamp, his face in a rash, "I won't have any of that in my bunkhouse."

"Tell him," said Dunbar. "He made the first move."

"You stood up and taunted him."

"You're half-right. I stood up."

Kelso rolled over onto all fours, picked up his knife from the floor, and rose to his feet. He was wearing his gun, but he did not touch it.

His eyes were hard, a mixture of resentment and caution, as he pulled himself together. His chest went up and down with a long breath, and his voice came out slow, with more of an accent than usual. "I'll finish wot I was saying, and I'll tell you only wonce. The way things work here, I give the orders. No one has to like it. But they do wot I say. In your case you pack your stuff and git out. Now."

"Fine with me. I've seen enough."

"And said enough, too."

I thought, there he was, getting in the last word again. I don't know what expression I had on my face, but he whipped his eyes on me, and I thought he was going to cuff me.

"You, too," he said. "You stand there with your teeth in your mouth, gawkin'."

I waited, still expecting him to try to hit me.

"Right now, you little son of a bitch. Roll your blankets. Get gone, just like your pal here."

"Tonight? I don't even have a horse to leave on."

"Then walk." Kelso turned to Dunbar and said, "You can pick up your wages at the Waverly Hotel." His glance brushed over me as he said, "The both of you."

Dusk was falling as Dunbar and I carried our belongings to the barn. My thoughts were going around and around, and I had no plan at all. But I was glad to get away from Kelso and the bunkhouse.

Dunbar did not sound discouraged. He sounded almost cheerful as he said, "I'm sorry he took it out on you. But that's the kind of fella he is."

"I'm sorry you lost your job so soon after you got it."

He laughed. "Given the circumstances, I'm surprised I lasted as long as I did. As you can tell, I don't mix with his kind at all. But you lost a real job, and now you're on foot. Don't worry, though. I think you can ride behind me. I'd let you ride my second horse, but I use a packsaddle on him. We'll get by."

"I don't want you to be stuck with me. I can make it on my own."

"It's no trouble. You can ride along with me."

"All the way to town tonight?"

"Oh, no. We can camp out. And I'd like to go to Carlyle's next, anyway."

★ ★ ★ ★ ★

A low haze hung on the distant mountains as the sky lightened in the east. Dunbar's voice had awakened me, and I saw that he was speaking to the picketed horses. The rest of the world lay quiet in the cool of morning.

I rolled out of my blankets, pulled on my boots, and reached for my hat. I was on my feet when Dunbar returned to camp.

"I don't think we'll have any coffee," he said. "I couldn't find a piece of dead sagebrush big enough to roast an ant. I do have some old biscuits, though."

"I won't complain. I'm sorry to be a burden anyway."

"Don't bother yourself about it. I'm the one who got us into this situation, and we won't be long getting out."

"I might have given you more of a warning about Kelso."

"You told me enough. And I had already taken my measure of him. As a general rule I don't get out of my chair that soon, but there are some things I don't have much tolerance for." Dunbar sniffed. "It's a weakness of mine. I want to see people treated with decency, even when I know the world is full of people who want to do the opposite."

"As far as that goes, I've heard Kelso use much worse language."

"I don't doubt it. Talk is cheap, in more than one sense of the word. They say actions speak stronger than words, but sometimes the talk itself is an action. It's a bad nature."

We rode into Tom Carlyle's place at midmorning. The barnyard came alive with the cackle of chickens and the squawk of ducks. From a pen out back, a chorus of *baa*-ing sheep joined in the racket. Two large white geese came forward to challenge us, hissing, while a trio of speckled guinea hens made low clucking sounds as they took their time getting out of the way of the horses' hooves.

I slid off the back of Dunbar's roan and kept an eye on the two geese. Dunbar held the lead rope clear and dismounted as well, and the geese turned away. The sheep quit crying. The rest of the din settled down except for one chicken, which sent up the same five-note scale over and over. Then it, too, went silent as the door of the farmhouse opened and Tom Carlyle stepped out.

He was dressed the same as the day before, and although his hat shaded his face, he squinted in the daylight.

"Good morning," he said. He frowned at each of us. "Did you come from Stanton's? You two were there yesterday, weren't you?"

"We were," said Dunbar. "But we don't work for that outfit anymore. Had a little difference with foreman Kelso."

Carlyle looked at each of us again. I could see he was weighing his words. "Something I can help you with?"

"Might be. We left on short notice, and this young man doesn't have a horse to ride." Dunbar motioned with his head toward the buckskin. "This horse rides all right, but I've got a packsaddle on him."

Carlyle opened his eyes. "Oh. Sure. I didn't notice. I hope you'll excuse me. I was up all night taking Ross to town, and I barely got an hour's sleep."

"Sorry for that. And sorry for what happened to Mr. Guilford."

"So am I. He was a good man. Gettin' on in years, but there was nothin' wrong with him."

"Still pretty able."

"I'd say so. He got around all right, and his mind was clear."

"Good with cattle."

"Oh, yes. Very good. I've got but twenty head, and he rode out every couple of days to keep an eye on 'em." Carlyle paused. "At one time, he was a good hand for any cattleman. He knew

31

how to breed up a herd, how to find cows when they calved in the out-of-the-way places, how to pull calves, how to keep 'em alive in bad weather. He knew what ailed a cow and how to doctor it."

"You said yesterday he was a natural on a horse."

"He was. And the horse I had him ride is as gentle as they come. My wife rides him. If a rider gets off balance, that horse will shift under 'em to keep 'em from falling off." Carlyle gave Dunbar a look of shared understanding. "You seemed to have your doubts yesterday, too, as I recall."

"I did."

Carlyle's eyes narrowed. "That's not why they let you go, is it?"

"Um, no. Kelso and I had a difference over something else, but for all I know, they may be related. He doesn't welcome other people's opinions."

Dunbar's comment sparked a thought in me. I had thought Kelso was being insistent about Ross Guilford having fallen off the horse, and I had sensed he was going out of his way to badger Willard, even the night before. Maybe the two were related.

Carlyle said, "Well, I didn't care for the way he regarded it."

"There could be more to know," said Dunbar. "Can you think of anyone else who might have an impression?"

Carlyle shrugged. "There's Jack Brumley, of course. He knew Ross for years." Carlyle looked at me. "You know where his place is. South of here, on the way to town."

"Sure," I said.

"We were planning to go that way," said Dunbar. "Which brings us to another small matter. Would you have a horse we might rent for Whit to ride?"

"There's the horse that Ross rode, but I wouldn't rent him out. I'll lend him to you, though, and if anyone wants to return the favor, I've always got work to do."

"Fine with me," I said. "And I thank you very much."

"I'll bring him out."

Carlyle headed for the barn, and I followed. I waited outside, under the watchful eyes of the two geese, which were now in the shade of an elm tree. Carlyle crossed through the dark interior, and a square of light showed as he opened a door to a corral in back. A minute later, he came out leading a medium-built palomino about fifteen hands high.

"His name's Sunny. Here's a brush. I'll get a saddle and bridle."

I recognized the horse, as I had seen Ross Guilford riding him on a few occasions. I patted Sunny on the neck and started slow with the brushing. The horse stood still as I ran the brush in longer sweeps. Carlyle returned with a saddle and bridle and set them on a nearby hitching rail, then handed me a steel comb. I finished with the brush and began to comb the light-colored mane.

Carlyle stood by and watched as I combed the mane and tail, put the saddle blankets in place, laid the saddle on top, cinched it, slipped the bit into the horse's mouth, and settled the headstall over the ears.

"Take good care of him," Carlyle said.

"I will."

"He took good care of Ross."

I led the horse out a dozen steps, tightened the cinch one hole, and swung aboard. I turned and waved. "Thanks again. We'll be back."

Dunbar was mounted on the blue roan with the buckskin in tow. As we rode out of the yard, he said, "I imagine this is the way to Jack Brumley's."

"It is." I was paying attention to the palomino beneath me. I had a haunted feeling of riding a dead man's horse, and I recalled the general rule of never trusting a horse one hundred percent. But Sunny felt steady and dependable, as if we had ridden together a dozen times.

Dunbar spoke again. "What can you tell me about him?"

I looked up. "Jack? He's about fifty, I'd guess. Has a small place of his own. You wouldn't know it to look at him, but he's Willard's father."

"Uh-huh."

I had the feeling, as I had had before, that I was telling Dunbar something he already knew. "Their place has never made much, I guess. Jack used to work for other ranches, and now Willard does."

"I see. And the wife?"

"The story is, she left about twenty years ago."

"That's why Kelso never saw her."

"Correct. Willard would have been five or six at the time."

"That's too bad. It's not easy for a boy to grow up without a mother."

"I know. I did the same thing."

Dunbar gave me what I thought was a sincere look. "I'm sorry to hear that. Not to be too personal, but did she die?"

"No. She went away. Left me. Unlike Willard, though, I didn't have a father to raise me. He left earlier."

Dunbar nodded. "That's a rough go."

I had the sense that he had some similar experience of growing up alone, but before I could form a question, he did.

"This was all in Ohio, then?"

"That's right." I met his eyes. "I never breathed a word of it to Kelso or Stanton or any of them."

Dunbar shook his head. "Just as well." As if to change the subject, he said, "It seems as if you got an education, though."

"I was lucky. A farm couple took me in. They got plenty of work out of me, but I was able to finish school."

"Time well spent. I've known lads who couldn't read a newspaper or even a thermometer."

"It set well with me, anyway. School did. I realize not every-one cares for it." Thinking we had talked enough about myself, I said, "I understand you're from the North."

"That's true."

"True north?"

"Ha-ha. You can't get any closer than that. But back to the topic we were on a while ago."

I nodded for him to continue.

"I'd like to know whether Kelso has, or had, anything against Ross Guilford or any of the Brumleys—aside from the obvious dislike of people who aren't like him."

"I've thought and thought about it since yesterday, and all I can come up with is that according to Slater, Willard made a comment a while back, and Kelso might have heard it. The gist of it was that the old man, Ross Guilford, had said he knew something. Nothing more specific than that."

"It's not much, but there might be something to it. People die for knowing things. By the way, how do you like that horse?"

"Nice as can be. Just goes to show that not all granger horses are crowbait."

"Gentle enough for his wife to ride. What's she like?"

"German, I believe. I haven't seen her. But they say she makes beer."

"Now that's a good girl. I saw that he had a potato cellar. I'd bet that's where she keeps the beer. Maybe we'll find out."

Jack Brumley's place consisted of a huddle of weathered build-ings—a house, a barn, and a couple of shacks, all made of lumber. Not a shade tree or bush grew in the yard, and the only sound came from a horse kicking a corral plank.

Dunbar called, "Anybody home?" When no one answered, he called again.

The blue roan snuffled, and all three of our horses looked toward the back of the house. A man came into view and gave a short wave of the hand. I recognized him as Jack Brumley, and I waved back.

My first thought was that he was showing his age. He wore an old, dove-colored hat with breaks in the brim and the crown, and his graying hair hadn't been trimmed in a while. His collarless, two-button shirt verged on being grimy. His stomach protruded past his open vest and caused his belt to sag. He walked with an uneven gait like a man whose feet hurt. Halfway to us, he reached his right arm across his chest and scratched his shoulder.

Dunbar and I dismounted. As Jack drew closer, I noted his tired brown eyes and his small, round red nose. He had about a three-day stubble that gave him a jowly look.

"What do you need?" he asked.

Dunbar spoke. "We thought we'd drop in and visit. We've had the pleasure of talking with your neighbor, Tom Carlyle, and he recommended that we meet you."

Jack motioned with his chin in my direction. "I think I know this one. Don't you work for Rich Stanton?"

"I did. Mr. Dunbar and I had a falling-out with Kelso, so we're free lances at the moment."

Jack drew his brows together. "That's the horse that Ross Guilford used to ride, isn't it?"

"Yes, it is. Tom Carlyle lent it to me." I mustered a little courage and said, "Did you hear about Ross, then?"

"Willard came by and told me yesterday evening." Jack's eyes moved toward Dunbar and back to me. "What did you have a falling-out with Kelso over? Not that it would take much."

I hesitated. "Willard might tell you that story as well, but I'll give you a short version. Kelso was riding Willard about one thing and another, and Mr. Dunbar expressed his opinion. Kelso tried to punch Mr. Dunbar, but he ended up on the floor. So he fired us."

"Kelso's a shit-face. I wish Willard would quit that outfit, but the wages help us hold things together. No secret about that. Things have always been that way. I had to work out for years, and now Willard does."

Dunbar said, "We were there when they found Ross Guilford."

Jack's tired eyes turned toward Dunbar. "You were?"

"Yes, and I can't say that things looked right."

"That's what Willard said."

"Now that I'm out of a job, a free lance as Whit calls me— and thanks for the poetic term, by the way—I've taken an interest in the case."

"Ross was a good man. If there's anything not right about the way he ended, I'd like to see it be known."

"So would I." Dunbar gave a slow, confidential nod.

Jack took off his hat and rubbed his shirt sleeve across his bald forehead, where beads of sweat had gathered. He put his hat back on. After a full breath, he said, "Ross was a quiet, polite fellow who kept to himself. He was the kind who would turn into an old bachelor, which he did."

"As far as you know, did he ever do anything to give someone a reason to—well, lift a hand against him?"

Jack shook his head. "No. He worked for wages. He never skinned anyone on a deal because he didn't go in for tradin' or dealin' and all of that. And he never so much as looked at another man's woman."

"Anything he might have said?"

Jack's eyebrows went up. "Now there's a puzzle. If there's anything, it's what he *wouldn't* say."

Dunbar gave a quizzical expression. "I don't follow you."

"Like I said, Ross minded his own business. But one time,

many years ago, he said to me, 'I could tell you something, Jack, but I won't.' I figured, from the way he said it, that it had something to do with my wife. And it was at a time when I worked for other outfits, like I said, and I was away from home for stretches of a week or more. Not too long after he told me that, she left. That's no secret, either. But I never found out what it was he wouldn't tell me, and I never knew who she left with."

Dunbar said, "Well, I'm sorry to hear that. It's a hard thing for a man to take, and Willard must have had a difficult life, growing up without a mother."

Jack heaved a sigh. His eyes relaxed, and the dark bags were noticeable in his lower eyelids. "It hasn't been easy on either of us, that's for sure. But it all happened a long time ago, and there's nothing any of us can do about it. We've just had to live with it."

"You've still got my sympathy."

"Thanks." Jack paused, and his eyes misted. "Louise was a good woman. I've imagined she had a reason for leaving. For years I hoped she would come back, but little by little, I gave up that hope. I think it's been even rougher on Willard. It's made him bitter. If you know Willard, you can see what I mean."

"I've met him." After a pause, Dunbar said, "Is Louise a French name?"

"In her case, yes. She was Creole. One part of her family was 'Cadian."

"Oh, yes. The Acadians. French people who were moved from Nova Scotia, New Brunswick, and that area to Louisiana. Quite a while back."

"That's them."

"Well, it's all interesting. The history. But, before I forget, I had a question about Ross Guilford's, what shall I call it, incomplete message."

"Go ahead."

"Did your son, Willard, know about it?"

"Yes. I told him when I thought he was old enough."

"Do you think Ross ever told him any more?"

"I don't think so, or he would have told me. I don't think he has ever known anything more than what I told you—that Ross said he could tell me something but he wouldn't." Jack took off his hat and mopped his pale forehead again. "Would you like to go inside? Get out of the sun?"

"We don't want to take up too much of your time."

"Don't worry about me. But I don't mind having a drink about this time of the day. You're welcome to join me." He glanced at me and nodded.

"No, thanks," said Dunbar. "We've still got to ride to town, and I don't care to drink and then go out into the hot sun."

"Neither do I."

"Don't let us hold you up anymore, then. But before you go, can you think of anyone else who could tell me about Ross Guilford?"

"Huh. If you're going into Dry Camp, you might look up an old drunk named Ambrose Lennox. He worked for the livery stable for years, and he was a friend of Ross and others in the old days."

"Thanks. That's good to know. Thanks for all your help. It's been good to meet you and visit with you."

"The same to you. When you come by this way again, don't be afraid to drop in. I can always use the company."

CHAPTER THREE

Dunbar and I rode into the town of Dry Camp from the north. We turned right and headed west a couple of blocks toward the town well, as the sun was moving into the latter part of the afternoon and we hadn't watered the horses since we left Carlyle's. While the horses drank, I pumped fresh water. Dunbar took a tin cup from his pack, rinsed it, and offered me the first cupful.

In the heat of the afternoon, as I lifted my hat to let the air circulate and cool my brow, I gazed at the west. Less than fifty yards away, a large white house, built up off the ground, was beginning to cast its afternoon shadow. The main floor of the house rested on a basement foundation that rose four feet above ground level. Outside the back door, a terrace was built up to the same height. On each side of the overhang leading out of the back door, wisteria vines made a kind of arbor, about eight feet square. The branches wrapped around the support posts with a tenacity that I knew could strangle young trees. Here, they hung onto the posts and supported their drooping clusters of pale purple blossoms, shriveling now and giving way to pods.

On the south and west sides of the terrace, a lilac hedge gave some enclosure. The leaves were of a darker green than the wisteria, and the dead blooms had turned to dry, brown clusters. Overall, a thin layer of dust gave a dull hue to the vegetation.

The terrace itself was paved with yellowish sandstone, not quite as smooth as flagstone but pleasing to the eye because of the natural look. I had seen such sandstone here and there in the plains country, at the bases of bluffs and in places where the ground broke open, and so the pieces seemed in harmony here. On a spring day after a time of rain, I had seen a yellow cat lapping water out of a shallow puddle in one of the stones. On another fresh spring morning, I had seen Rich Stanton's wife and their two perfect daughters taking a meal in the arbor. Such days were rare, however, when the weather was not hot or cold or when there was no wind to raise the dust. Today, the puddles of water, the cat, the fresh spring day, and the impeccable woman and girls were all stored away in memory.

Dunbar seemed to be regarding the house with interest, which was normal, I thought, as it was more imposing than the other houses in town. He did not ask whose house it was, though, and I did not say anything.

After this brief moment, Dunbar put away the tin cup. We pulled the horses away from the water trough, tightened the cinches we had loosened, and mounted up. With our backs to the white house and the terrace baking in the sun, we headed into the older part of town.

"There's the Waverly Hotel," I said, as we approached it on our left.

Dunbar gave the building an appraising glance. "I doubt that they're ready for us yet. Do you know where this fellow Ambrose Lennox lives?"

"I think so. It's on the next street north, parallel to this one."

I turned left at the third cross street, then right on the next corner, and brought us to a shack in the middle of the block on the left. The wooden building sat on a bare, narrow lot and could not have been bigger than twelve feet by twenty-four. In the shade of a low-roofed front porch, Ambrose Lennox sat dozing.

At the sound of our horses stepping on the dry ground in

front of his house, he came awake and shook his head. He fixed a stare on us as we came to a halt.

"Are you Mr. Lennox?" asked Dunbar.

"Yes, I am." The old man stood up, took a step forward, and steadied himself with a hand on the post of his narrow porch.

If I had seen him two days before, I would not have bet that he would outlive Ross Guilford. He had thinning white hair, a pale scalp, a flushed face with broken blood vessels and a purple nose, brown eyes with yellowed whites, thin arms, a soft stomach, and a sagging belt. He wore an old, unwashed collarless shirt with frayed cuffs, and his trousers were ingrained with grime and dirt.

His eyes moved back and forth at both of us, and he raised himself with a breath. "What can I do for you?" he asked.

"My name's Dunbar. This is my young friend, Whit Barnett."

Lennox turned a jaundiced eye on me. "I've seen him before. And that looks like Ross Guilford's horse he's riding."

"On loan from Tom Carlyle," said Dunbar. "I suppose you've heard about what happened to Ross."

"Of course." The corners of the old man's mouth pointed down, and his expression did not show any trust.

"We're sorry for what happened. We were there when the body was found, and you might say we share Mr. Carlyle's skepticism."

The old eyes drifted back toward me. "I thought this one worked for old high-and-mighty."

"We both worked for Rich Stanton, up until yesterday. Mr. Kelso let us go."

"He did, huh? Well, maybe someday someone'll let him go."

"I didn't work there very long."

"Your good luck." Lennox gave a sharp sniff and then coughed. "So what did you come and see me for?"

"Jack Brumley said you might be able to tell us more about

your old friend Ross Guilford."

"What for? You're not some kind of a law man, are you?"

"No, but as I told Jack, I've taken some interest in the story, and I don't have any other claims on my time at the moment."

"You sound like a crusader. Last one who talked like that, he turned out to be a labor organizer. Sweet as a peach, on his way to blow things up in a mining town."

Dunbar laughed. "That's none of me," he said.

"But you come around snoopin'."

"That's all right," said Dunbar. "We don't want to impose on you. I understood that you were a man who knew a great deal about this town and some of its people, and I thought we might enjoy some conversation with you. But here we are, with the hot sun beatin' down on us, pestering you, when we should just as well go find a shady place. So we'll thank you for your time and be on our way."

"It *is* hot and dusty, and I never said I wouldn't talk to you."

With a half-smile, Dunbar said, "Perhaps you know of a place where the sun doesn't beat down so fierce."

"Perhaps I do." Lennox turned his yellowed eyes at me again. "If you boys want to meet me at the Dakota Rose, I'll be along right behind you."

Back to the center of town we rode. Lennox was not far behind, for my eyes were adjusting to the dark interior of the saloon when he walked in.

Dunbar made a motion with his arm and said, "Let's take a table."

The bartender brought Lennox a glass of whiskey without the old man saying a word. Dunbar ordered a glass of beer, and I did the same. When the glasses arrived, I was surprised at how cool the beer was.

Lennox did not stand on ceremony. He had two sips down the hatch by the time I had taken my first drink.

"Tell us about the town," said Dunbar. "And let me say, I'm glad it's not dry in the way that some places are."

"I wouldn't live in one of those towns. Of course, they wouldn't ask me to."

"There's a little good in everything. They don't have piles of empty bottles out in back of the buildings."

"Nah. They keep all their vices well hidden. That's respectability."

"Different towns have different versions," said Dunbar. After a few seconds, he spoke again. "Sometimes you wonder how a town came to be in a certain place."

"In the case of this town, it's a place where three trails come together. So it was a place where freighters stopped. When the men put in the first way station, they had to drill for water. They used one of those slow machines where a horse turns a wheel that turns a bit. They found enough water to supply a few people and keep a stock tank full. By common agreement, there were no trees or gardens. People kept things to the bare necessities. So the town didn't grow much. Then a fella came along, a water witcher, by the name of Malcolm Roach. This is a well-known story by now. He found water, good water, just a few hundred yards from where they drilled the old well. Now everyone could have trees and such." Lennox took a sip from his glass. "They dug this new well on the west edge of town, and all the newer houses and buildings were built on that side."

Dunbar said, "We stopped there on the way in. At the well."

"Made a big difference. It's still a little town out in the middle of nowhere, but it's not limited to a road house and a wagon yard."

"We saw one house that looked rather handsome. Right on the other side of the well there."

"That would be Stanton's house. I doubt that he'll invite you inside."

Dunbar shrugged. "Maybe I won't go knocking on his door. I didn't find him as hard to take as his foreman, though."

"I'd say that's normal."

Dunbar waited a couple of seconds and spoke again. "When I was out at the ranch, I understood that he had a house in town. I suppose he has a family."

"He's got a wife that you would think was chiseled from pure white marble. And two daughters to match."

I said their names to myself. *Diana* and *Lucinda*.

Dunbar said, "No wonder he built such a nice house."

"He built it when he was courting Agnes Rutledge."

"Oh. Was she from here?"

"Not to begin with. Her folks were from Iowa, and they came out here so her father could get in on the building of the town."

"And he's still here?"

"He is. The wife's dead. His name's Gilbert Rutledge, and he owns the Waverly Hotel." Lennox brought out a small white sack of tobacco and a sheaf of papers.

Dunbar said, "That's where we were told to pick up our wages."

"They're partners of sorts, Stanton and the old man. When Stanton is at the ranch, Rutledge handles some of his business."

Dunbar nodded. "Stanton keeps his business separate from his home life."

Lennox spilled a few grains of tobacco as he built his cigarette. I imagined he might have been more dexterous earlier in life, but my thoughts were cut short when he caught me watching him. "Not entirely," he said as he held up the cigarette and prepared to lick the edge of the paper. "The missus wants to make her house into some kind of a social center. Not for the high society of Dry Camp, of course, but for other cattlemen and their wives. She wants to add onto the house, to have a bigger sitting room and a formal dining room."

"To use once or twice a year?"

"I suppose." Lennox tapped his finger along the wet seam of his cigarette. "One of them must be hard to please, though, because one contractor after another has come in here, proposed a plan, and gone away."

Dunbar paused with his glass of beer in his hand. "The upper classes have different problems than we do." He took a drink, then waited for Lennox to strike a match. "You've lived here quite a while, then?"

"Well over twenty years." Lennox held the match to the end of his cigarette.

"Jack Brumley said you were friends with Ross Guilford and others, back in those earlier days."

Lennox puffed on his cigarette. "That I was. Most of 'em are dead and gone now, though. Even Ross."

"Everyone speaks well of him."

"He was the best." Lennox's eyes looked mournful as he breathed out a cloud of smoke. "He never went out of his way to say anything bad about anyone."

"Respectful of women."

"Oh, you bet. He held them in utmost respect. As if they lived in a different world than he did."

"Jack Brumley said just about the same thing."

"Jack's all right."

"Seems to be. Would you like another drink?"

"I wouldn't turn it down." Lennox took a sip.

Dunbar signaled to the bartender. Back to Lennox, he said, "That's a sad story about Jack's wife leaving."

"It was."

"Did you know her?"

"Louise? Not very well. They lived in the country. I met her several times, of course, but I didn't talk to her much." Lennox tipped his head. "We were all a lot younger then. People said one thing and another. Maybe she did walk out on her husband and son, but as far as I ever knew her, she was not half-bad. And Jack never had anything but good to say about her."

"Women are almost always a mystery," Dunbar said.

"Seems that way." Lennox's face brightened as the bartender set down a glass of whiskey. Lennox looked at me and said, "How about you?"

I saw that he was looking at my glass, which was more than halfway down. I was glad he wasn't asking me about girls. "I've got enough," I said.

Dunbar took a drink and lowered his glass. "I'll tell you, this whole thing has me curious." Bending his gaze in a relaxed way toward Lennox, he said, "Is there anyone else you can think of who might know more about your friend Ross, or even about Louise Brumley?"

Lennox pushed his empty glass aside and laid his thumb and fingers on the new one. "As for Ross, I can't think of anyone else at the moment. Like I said, a lot of the old friends have gone on." He took a small sip. "As for Louise, I think Jane Lancaster might have had some level of confidence with her." After what seemed to be a short reflection, he added, "I don't think she would have crossed paths very much with Ross. But she knew Louise." Lennox looked at me as he pointed over his shoulder with his thumb. "You know where she lives, don't you?"

"I think so," I said.

Out in the sunlight after sitting in a dark saloon, I felt my eyes strain, and I had to yawn. Dunbar was showing similar effects as he stretched his facial muscles and gave a shake of the head.

"Let's go to the well and wash our faces," he said. "Wake up a little."

At the water trough, we loosened the cinches and let the

horses drink again.

"You go first," said Dunbar.

He took hold of the handle and worked the pump as I tipped back my hat and splashed water on my face. The water was not as cool as if it were a mountain stream, but it felt good.

When I took my turn at the pump handle, Dunbar pulled off his gloves and set them on the seat of his saddle. He hung his hat on the saddle horn, squared his shoulders, and relaxed as he bent to his work. He cupped his hands beneath the spout and rinsed them, washed his face, and rinsed his hands again.

At that moment, I saw something I hadn't noticed before. A dark spot showed in the palm of his right hand, as if he had been burned there. The mark was more visible when it was wet, I suppose. Why I assumed he had been burned rather than scarred in some other way, I am not sure. But the spot was darker than a pink scar or a white one, and it was round. Also, I had read of transported felons from England and of slaves in the South who had been burned that way, and so it was as if I recognized the mark.

He did not seem to make any attempt to hide it. He splashed his face a second time, then stood up and squared his shoulders again as he waved his hands in the warm, dry air. He wore what seemed to me an expensive shirt, tan-colored, made of light canvas, with a collar, two chest pockets, and a full row of buttons. I appreciated his not wiping his hands on his shirt.

In this suspended moment, when the splashing of water had ended and neither of us had spoken, a faint noise drew our attention to the raised terrace of the Stanton house. Through the small arbor of wisteria vines, a white figure moved. I recognized Agnes Stanton as she stepped into the sunlight. Her blond hair was tied up and pinned, and she wore a white dress trimmed in yellow. She moved in a light, smooth motion, as if her feet barely touched the paving stones. At the far end of the terrace, she shook out a white napkin. She turned with perfect composure and glided back to the arbor and into the house. Two birds of the sparrow or finch variety fluttered down to pick at the crumbs.

A retaining wall of stone, matching the foundation of the house, held the terrace about four feet above ground level. The word "eminence" came to mind as I gazed at what seemed like an elevated earthen stage. Yet I was certain that Mrs. Stanton did not make her appearance for our benefit but would have waited if she had realized we groundlings were there to watch.

A voice from behind us broke the silence.

"Well, hello, young men. And here we meet at the well."

I turned to see a familiar figure in a flat-crowned hat, a dark suit, a white shirt, thin suspenders, and polished shoes that the man did not seem to be afraid of getting dusty.

"Good afternoon, Reverend," I said. I took off my hat and said, "I don't believe you know Mr. Dunbar."

"Not yet." The minister held forward a pale hand with prominent blue veins on the back of it. "I'm Reverend Mansfield. Most people call me Preacher. I answer to that. It's a pleasure to meet you."

"And the same for me," said Dunbar. "Would you like a drink of water? I've got a tin cup in my pack, and it's my turn to work the handle."

The reverend smiled. Slender, pale, clean-shaven, and deep-eyed, he had an easy way about him in a world of harsh sun and wind, as well as rough men who rode in from the range. "What I would like," he said, "is a glass of living water. Do you know what I mean?"

Dunbar smiled in return. "I don't remember it, chapter and verse."

"When Jesus meets the woman at the well, he says he would give her living water. He says, 'Whosoever drinketh of the water that I shall give him shall never thirst; but the water that I shall give him shall be in him a well of water springing up into everlasting life.' Perhaps you remember it now."

"The woman was Samaritan, as I recall."

"Jesus was in Samaria, yes. And the Samaritans did not have much to do with the Jews. The woman had had five husbands and was living with a man she wasn't married to, and still Jesus spoke truly with her."

Dunbar said, "It's a good story, with more than one lesson in it." He moved toward his horse, retrieved his hat and gloves, and stood with them in his hands.

The reverend gave a light laugh. "Put on your hat, young man. The sun is strong, and the sermon is ended."

"Thank you, Reverend. For sharing the lesson from Scripture, as well."

"All in a day's work. I've seen heedless, godless men blown in off this land, and even they have their spiritual needs at times. If such a moment comes to you, I'm not hard to find." He touched his brim. "Good day."

We returned the courtesy and watched him walk away, back to the older part of town.

Dunbar spoke as he pulled on his gloves, "We'll give him a couple of minutes so we don't ride over the top of him." He motioned with his head. "I gathered that Jane Lancaster lives in one of the houses over that way."

"She does."

"We've got time. What can you tell me about her?"

"Let's see. Where to begin? She's a bit older, maybe the age of Ambrose Lennox, maybe a little younger. I've heard her referred to as Mrs. Lancaster, but she's either a widow or long separated, for I've never heard of a Mr. Lancaster. Nor any children. And she doesn't have much of a feminine presence. She keeps her hair cut short, wears drab clothes."

Dunbar gave a wry smile. "As opposed to the woman at the well, who had five husbands."

I shrugged. "I was just describing her."

"I know. Go ahead. How does she get by? Does she work at something?"

"From what I understand, she's been a midwife."

"Well, now," said Dunbar. "There's a person who might know something. I'm sure a person in her line of work sees and hears things the rest of us never will." Dunbar patted the nose of the blue roan. I didn't know if he was speaking to me or to the horse when he said, "What do you think? Shall we give it a try?"

All three horses had been standing relaxed with their heads lowered and their muzzles damp. They perked up as we led them into the street, where we snugged the cinches and climbed aboard.

I led us back through town for four blocks and turned right. A block later, I drew rein in front of a house on our left. "This is it," I said.

We swung down, and Dunbar handed me his reins and the lead rope. I stood with the three horses as he walked up the pathway to the little house. After he knocked a couple of times, the door opened.

From a short distance, Jane Lancaster appeared as I had recalled her—a slender woman, not very tall, in a loose dress and apron. She had straight, gray hair, not well trimmed, that didn't cover her ears. A small red nose and a pair of dark eyes showed against her pale complexion.

I did not pick up any specific words as she and Dunbar spoke in an exchange of a few short sentences each. Then the door closed as Dunbar turned and began to walk toward me.

I handed him the reins and the lead rope, and the two of us walked back toward the center of town. When we reached the main street, we paused.

"No luck today," said Dunbar. "She's not interested in talking to me." He looked up and down the street, where a couple of horses stood tied to hitching rails but no people were in sight. "I can't blame her, though. To her, I'm just a stranger." He shrugged. "Maybe another time."

"What next?" I asked.

"I suppose we could drop in at the Waverly Hotel."

CHAPTER FOUR

We made our way to the Waverly Hotel in less than ten minutes. It sat on the north side of the main street, about one block east of the town well. Two stories, it stood on a corner lot with a roofed front porch. The building was freshly painted a grayish-blue with red trim, and the flower beds on each side of the front steps had an array of white, red, pink, violet, and purple petunias. As I swung down from Sunny, I imagined such an extravagance as being unthinkable in the early days of Dry Camp.

Our boot heels echoed as we walked up the plank steps and across the wooden porch. The large pane of glass on the front door lay in shadow. The name of the hotel, in red script, took up the center of an oval of clear glass, while the area outside the oval was frosted. Our reflections were fragmented, and I could not see in, though I imagined someone inside could see out.

A bell jingled as we opened the door and went in. A rug on the hardwood floor muffled our steps in the calm, quiet interior. The air was fifteen or twenty degrees cooler than outside, and the afternoon glare was shaded out. Across the lobby, a reception desk of polished oak contributed to the atmosphere of civility.

Behind the desk, or counter, a man stood up and faced us. By his features, I recognized him as the proprietor of the hotel. He was taller than average and silver-haired. He wore a sky-blue suit that, as we drew closer, brought out the blue of his eyes. He was clean-shaven with a clear complexion, and he put on his business smile as he addressed us.

"Gentlemen. How may I help you?"

Dunbar answered. "The foreman at the Clay Creek Ranch told us we could pick up our wages here."

"Ah, yes. And you are—?"

"J.R. Dunbar."

"Whit Barnett."

"Yes. I'm Gilbert Rutledge, of course. I was told you might drop by, but I must tell you I haven't gotten your time yet. I should have it later in the day."

"I see," said Dunbar. "Mine doesn't amount to much, but Whit's will be a little more. And whatever the amount, I understand you want it to be accurate."

"Exactly." Rutledge gave Dunbar what seemed like a look of appraisal. "I'm sorry your job didn't last long, but I realize that not everyone gets along with my son-in-law's foreman. I try to stay out of it, but even at a distance, I can't help knowing that much."

Dunbar nodded. "Sometimes things don't work out. It's more of an inconvenience for Whit than it is for me, but either of us is capable of finding another job."

Rutledge looked at me, and with less deference in his voice, he said, "I've seen you before, haven't I?"

"Yes. I've been working at the ranch for a couple of months, and I've been to town a few times."

"Well, however much you have coming, you'll get it. Rich is fair, I'll say that." His eyes moved back to Dunbar. "I'd say, come back in another couple of hours."

The sound of a heavy-footed person on the stairway caused the three of us to look around. A man wearing a loose-fitting, brownish-gray coat and pants thumped down the last two steps and paused. He had a full build and a full face, with straight brown hair and a bristly mustache. In his hand he carried a brown hat with a domed crown. He settled the hat onto his head, smiled, and stepped forward. He handed his room key to Rutledge.

The proprietor said, "Thanks, Pat."

"I'll be back later." The man nodded to each of us and walked out of the hotel.

"We'll be back, too," said Dunbar. "Pleased to meet you."

"Likewise."

Out on the street, Dunbar said, "I don't know if it has occurred to you, but we haven't eaten since this morning."

"I can't say I didn't notice. I'm pretty hungry."

"I noticed Mr. Rutledge has a dining room, but as a matter of principle, at least at this point, I'd rather have money flowing in only one direction with those people."

"I agree."

"Do you happen to know of another place?"

"There's the Deville Café. I've been there only once, but the food was all right and the prices were modest."

"That sounds good to me. How far is it?"

"About four blocks down on our left. Just past the street we turned on to go to Mrs. Lancaster's house."

"Then we'll take the horses."

As we rode down the main street for the third time that afternoon, dragging the packhorse, I felt as if everyone in town had gotten a good look at us. Dunbar seemed unconcerned, however. He rode easy in the saddle, with a light expression on his face, as he whistled a soft version of "Red River Valley."

We tied up at the hitching rail in front of the café and went in. Late afternoon was about to give way to early evening, and the interior of the place had a deserted feel such as cafés sometimes do at that hour.

The tinkle of the doorbell faded as a woman in a white blouse and a black skirt came out of the kitchen area. Her eyebrows went up as she saw us, and she smiled.

"Good evening, gentlemen. Would you like a table?"

"It would be an honor," said Dunbar.

She gave him a sideways glance as she walked around the counter and finished wiping her hands on a cloth. "Over here?" She led the way to a table where we had a view of the street but would not be sitting in the window. As we took our seats, she struck a pose with one foot forward and her hands on her hips.

She had a striking appearance. She had dark, wavy, shoulder-length hair, and her eyes shined like black cherries. Her tan complexion and red lips made a pleasing contrast with her white blouse. She had a shapely figure, not of a girl but of a woman. I guessed her age at about thirty, which seemed old to me, but I could see why a man like Dunbar would find her attractive.

Her eyes sparkled as he looked up at her and said, "Do you have a main dish this evening?"

"Roast beef with potatoes and gravy."

"Sounds irresistible."

"It's fresh-cooked for this evening. No leftovers."

"I'll have it, then. And you, Whit?"

"I'll have the same."

"Very good." She tipped her head and walked away. My back was turned to that direction, but I could see that the effect was not lost on Dunbar.

He offered no comment as we waited for our meal. He took off his hat and set it on the chair next to him, so I did the same. No other customers came into the café, so we were alone when the woman returned with our two plates. She put mine down and then his.

Dunbar's eyes met hers as he said, "Thank you."

I repeated the courtesy, feeling awkward for not having said it first.

"You're welcome," she said. "I'll be back with the coffee."

She returned in a couple of minutes with a coffeepot and two cups. As she poured the coffee, she said, "How is your meal?"

Dunbar and I spoke at once. "Very good."

"I'm glad you like it." She stood with one hand on her hip as she held the coffeepot with the other. "I should mention that we do have pie as well."

Dunbar's eyebrows went up. "Do you?"

"Yes. All we have today is rhubarb. Let me know if you'd like some."

"I can put in a word for it right now," he said.

"Two?" She looked at me.

"Sure."

She left us to finish our meal. When she brought the servings of pie, she said, "On other days, we have other kinds. Apple, and sometimes peach."

"That's good to know," said Dunbar. "It'll give us a reason to come back."

"By all means."

"I'm partial to both."

When we were finished with dessert and presented ourselves at the cash register, Dunbar insisted on paying for both meals. I stood back as he made the transaction. Through the opening to the kitchen area, I caught a glimpse of a dark-haired girl in a white apron. My pulse jumped as her eyes flickered, and she moved out of sight.

"And do come back," said the woman who waited on us.

"We will. My name's Dunbar, and this is my young friend, Whit."

She smiled at each of us, but more at him. "My name's Medora."

"A great pleasure to meet you," he said.

"And I'm pleased to meet both of you."

Out on the street, we walked with the three horses toward the center of town. Dunbar glanced around and said, "Medora. Do you think her last name is Deville?"

"I believe it is. I understand she's the owner."

"Miss Deville, or Mrs.?"

"Mrs. Deville, as I've heard."

"Does her husband run the kitchen, then?"

"I don't think so. From what I've heard, she's a widow."

"A young widow." Then, as if to amend himself, he said, "Nothing wrong with that, of course."

An image of the girl in the kitchen stayed in my mind as we walked along the street. I did not know if Dunbar had seen her, but he did not miss much. Either way, I was glad he did not mention her. I had learned that older men had a tendency to needle younger men about girls and such matters, probably because they themselves had been teased and it was now their turn to dish it out, and I was glad that Dunbar was not so forward.

As we were passing the Dakota Rose, a voice hailed us from the shadowed doorway.

"Hey, you punchers. I see you're still in town."

As we stopped, I recognized the slack posture and pale features of Ambrose Lennox.

Dunbar called back, "I thought you went home."

"I did, but I usually come down here at this time of day. Are you in too big of a hurry to join me?"

"We've got a little time, I suppose. Is there anything special?"

"I've got a question I want to ask you, and I don't want to shout it in the street."

"Well, we wouldn't want you to." Dunbar turned to me and winced his eyebrows. "Shall we?"

"Might as well. Rutledge said to come back in a couple of hours, and it's been less than one."

We tied the horses to the hitching rail as Lennox stood in the open doorway with his eyes drooping and a relaxed smile on his face.

"Hah, hah," he said as we stepped up onto the sidewalk. "I didn't know when I'd see you again."

He led the way in a shuffling gait to the table where we had sat earlier. When we were seated and the bartender had delivered our drinks, Lennox leaned toward Dunbar and said, "So I hear you gave Kelso a thumpin'. Good for you."

"How did you hear that?"

"Sagebrush telegraph. One fella tells another."

Dunbar shrugged. "Maybe that means we'll get paid. Rutledge was waiting for someone to tell him how much time we had coming. I can't imagine Stanton spreading that kind of news, though."

Lennox bobbed his head with an open-mouthed smile. "He wouldn't have to. Something like that doesn't stay a secret."

Dunbar said, "Well, it was a small thing."

"Enough to get the two of you fired."

"I think he overdid it when he fired Whit, but that's done now, so it doesn't matter."

"Yeah, but I would've liked to have been there to see it." Lennox waved his fist. "The old sockdolager."

Dunbar gave a backward wave of the hand. "Don't make too much of it."

The light at the doorway shifted as a man walked through. I recognized the plodding steps and then the full build of the man we had seen handing in his key at the Waverly Hotel.

Lennox called out to him. "Hey, you old mud-dauber. What are you doin'?"

As the man walked toward our table, I saw that his heavy

step came from shifting his weight from one side to another. He came to a stop next to Lennox and clapped the older man on the shoulder. "What about you, you old jaybird? What sort of lies are you tellin' these two honest fellas?"

"I don't tell lies. Why aren't you out workin'?"

"I'm done for the day. I came in here for one drink before supper."

"You're in a hurry, then."

"Not at all." The man reached up and tipped his hat as he smiled at Dunbar and me. "Name's Hendy. Pat Hendy. I believe I saw you two gents earlier." He set the hat back on his head. The domed crown matched him well.

"My name's Dunbar."

"And mine is Whit Barnett."

"Pat's a busy beaver," said Lennox.

Dunbar gave an open expression. "Is that right?"

"Workin' on it," said Hendy. "I've been takin' measurements and drawin' up plans to do some work for Mrs. Stanton. That's how I come to be put up at the Waverly."

"I see," said Dunbar.

"Yes, sir. Mrs. Stanton doesn't want anything less than the best, and if we're going to do something, we're going to do it right."

"You have workmen, then?"

"Not here, but I know where I can get 'em. That's after I have the go-ahead, of course. I'm just in the plannin' stage right now."

I rather appreciated the fellow and his self-confidence. He did not show any awareness of other men having been turned away from the work, but for all I knew, he had heard of every one of them and had smiled.

The bartender came and went, and a glass of beer appeared in Hendy's hand. He took a drink and, standing with his feet planted, he held forth. "Lotta work. We'll have to yank out the lilac bushes and those strangling wisteria vines, take out the retaining walls, grade away that raised bed of dirt, and dig footings for a foundation on three sides and one down the middle."

"That *is* a lot of work," said Dunbar.

"It's just the beginning, and nothing I can't handle. As for the bushes and all, that's nothin'. I've blown out tree stumps bigger'n anything you'll ever see in this part of the country. As for the dirt, I've moved banks and mounds and hills of it that a whole army of Egyptians would hang their jaws at."

"With your own crew of workmen."

"You bet." Hendy quaffed about a fourth of his glass, and with his eyes relaxed on Dunbar, he said, "What sort of work do you do?"

"I'm a cowpuncher."

"I wouldn't have guessed otherwise." Hendy moved his glass in a merry little motion. "But, you know, every man, or at least every good man, has it in him to be more than one thing. Me, if I wasn't a builder, I could be doin' somethin' way different." He turned to me and beamed a smile. "Like runnin' a dance hall with a string of chorus girls."

"We could use some of them here," said Lennox.

Our group's attention was diverted by the appearance of another man in the doorway. I could see nothing but silhouette until he moved to the bar, where the light of a single lamp made him visible. He ordered a drink, exchanged a few words with the bartender, and walked over to our table.

He was of middle height, slender, with a hook nose, narrow eyes with puffy lower lids, and a muddy, freckled complexion. He wore a big gray shirt and a loose-hanging yellowish vest; a light-brown hat with a round, ridged crown; a dull-brown gun-belt and holster with a yellow-handled revolver; and brown boots with no spurs. He came to a stop between Hendy and

Dunbar, and with an intense look in his blue-gray eyes, he spoke to Dunbar.

"I understand you work for Mr. Stanton."

"Not anymore," said Dunbar.

The stranger pivoted on his boot heel and tossed a glance at the barkeep.

"Not him. The other one."

Turning back, and leaning forward, he said to Hendy, "Do you?"

"Work for Mr. Stanton? Well, yes and no. I'm doing some work to see about doing some work for him. I'm a builder, and I'm drawing up plans for a job."

The stranger looked Hendy up and down. "When do you think you'll see him?"

"Sometime tomorrow, I imagine."

"That's not very soon."

Hendy took a drink and seemed to make an effort in swallowing. "If it's a message or something like that, I could pass it on. If not to him, at least to his—well, to someone who's likely to see him."

The stranger settled his eyes on Hendy. "That would be fine. My name's Holcomb. I came to see about doin' some work for him, too, but it's at the ranch."

Lennox flinched.

Holcomb turned and said, "Somethin' botherin' you, pop?"

"Oh, no," said the old man. "As far as the ranch goes, he probably needs help. I heard a couple of men left."

Holcomb returned to Hendy. "If it's not too much trouble."

"None at all. I'm on my way to the Waverly in a couple of minutes. I'll leave word there. He's connected, you know."

"I didn't. But thanks." Holcomb nodded to the rest of the table and walked back to the bar.

Hendy's features relaxed as he broke into a smile. "Say, are you the two fellas who left the ranch?"

As we nodded, I appreciated his not saying Stanton's name out loud. Otherwise, he did not seem daunted.

"Well, if you're both out of work, who knows? I might have some work before long. Don't worry. You'd be workin' for me, not him. You wouldn't have to cross paths."

Dunbar answered. "We'll see. We might have some other work to do."

Hendy's round hat bobbed as he nodded. "We'll keep it open. Meanwhile, I'd best be going." He downed the rest of his beer, shook Dunbar's hand and then mine, patted Lennox on the shoulder, and took leave of the bartender on the way out.

"Nice fellow," said Lennox.

Dunbar motioned with his head. "He paid for all our drinks."

"How do you know?"

"I heard him. I think you were paying attention to something else."

Lennox gave a sideways look and spoke in a low voice. "I was. It's that newcomer. I've heard of him before. He's been in and out of all the railroad towns." Lennox spoke even lower. "They call him Holcomb the Hawk."

"Don't let it trouble you," said Dunbar. "He's got no quarrel with any of us. Not yet, anyway."

We presented ourselves at the Waverly Hotel at nightfall. Light was spilling onto the front porch, and a few insects of the night were gathering on the window panes.

As we entered, the sound of the doorbell died away, and an undertone of voices carried from the dining room on our left. Straight ahead, Mr. Rutledge's head was visible where he sat behind the reception desk. To our right, a gladstone bag stood alone in front of a vacant davenport and not far from a silent piano.

At our approach, Gilbert Rutledge stood up, bringing into view his silver hair and sky-blue suit. He had an air of familiarity as he smiled and said, "Good evening, gentlemen. It's a pleasure to see you again."

"As it is for us," said Dunbar.

Rutledge's eyes lowered as he reached below the level of the counter. "I'm glad to say that your time came in." Raising his head and smiling again, he set a silver dollar on the oak top. "Yours is not very much, of course."

Dunbar said, "That much is welcome. Thanks."

In another smooth motion, Rutledge put four five-dollar gold pieces and three silver dollars on the counter in front of me. "I trust that the amount is correct," he said.

"Yes, it is." I picked up the coins and put them in my pocket.

"Very well." Rutledge turned to Dunbar. "As I said before, I'm sorry your work didn't last longer. I assure you there are no hard feelings—except on Kelso's side, perhaps—and a man can be forgiven for not getting along with him." A shine in Rutledge's blue eyes suggested to me that he had heard about the fight and had formed a favorable impression.

"I'm happy to leave it behind," said Dunbar.

"That's the best way." Rutledge drew a full breath. "Depending on what your interests are for future work, I have a thought I'll mention."

"Go ahead."

Rutledge looked to either side but did not lower his voice. In a plain, businesslike tone, he said, "My son-in-law and I have an enterprise we'd like to start. You might call it a speculation."

Dunbar nodded for him to go ahead.

"It's about ten miles south of here. We plan to lay out a township."

"Like this one?"

"Not exactly. We hope to find water, of course. But the key is

in its location. It lies along the route where a rail line is supposed to be going through in the next couple of years."

"The speculation, then, as you call it, is to buy the land,
divide it into parcels, and sell the lots."

"That's the idea. I've already bought the land, and I've got a
name for the town."

"Oh."

"Madeleine. It was my wife's name, you see."

Dunbar assumed a tone of reverence. "It's a touching tribute,
sir."

"It's as much for my daughter and my grand-daughters as it
is for my late wife."

"It seems very fitting." After a respectable pause, Dunbar
said, "How far along is your project?"

"Like I said, we've got the land. A full section. Square mile.
I'd like to get started on the layout and parceling. But that's
down there, and I'm here. And Rich is busy as can be. If I'm
going to have men with instruments and equipment crawling
over my property, I'd like to have someone keep an eye on
things." He glanced my way. "And help out as needed."

Dunbar spoke. "I can't say right now. We've got another possibility to look at, so we couldn't know for a few days. Maybe a
week."

Rutledge nodded. "Give it a thought. That's plenty of time
for me. Things don't happen overnight."

"Good enough," said Dunbar. "We'll be on our way. We'll
talk to you again before long."

"Very well. And good evening."

Out on the street with the horses, I said to Dunbar, "What
other work do we have to look into?"

"We need to go back to Carlyle's. While we're at it, we'll see
if he needs any help. He could probably use it, since he just lost
his hired man. Of course, we need to give him back his horse.

And in order to do that, we need to find something else for you to ride. Unless you want to stay here. I can take the horse back."

I had been assuming I would have to buy a horse at some point, but I hadn't planned on seeing my earnings disappear so soon. I said, "I'll go along. I'm leery about buying a horse, though. Will you help me? Pick one out, that is."

"If I see one you shouldn't buy, I'll find some way to warn you before you throw away your money. Otherwise, it's your deal."

"It's a big step for me. But I know I should have my own horse."

"Sure. Then you're free to go whenever you want."

We put up our horses at the livery stable, across the street from the Waverly Hotel. From there we walked two blocks to a lodging house run by a man named Hunton.

The proprietor met us at the door and welcomed us. He had a nose like a misshapen sausage and a protruding stomach that threatened to break the buttons on his vest. I had seen him before, but this was the first time I had heard him speak. He had a quack in his voice, but he did not tell us where he came from. He told us he had had two wives who had died. He had fought in the Indian wars before that. He was no relation to the Hunton who was so well known in the area up around Chugwater and Fort Laramie. We were the only ones staying at his place that night. He would serve breakfast in the morning. No one was allowed to smoke in the rooms because he did not want to burn the place down. He had seen a sign once that read, "If you smoke in bed, tell us where to send your ashes." He didn't want to give anyone that opportunity.

We took a room that had two cots and a little stand between them. The air was heavy, so Hunton opened a window that looked out upon a dead wall four feet away.

He said, "I don't think I need to tell you fellas, but we don't have anyone comin' in or goin' out through that window, either."

"I'll keep an eye on it," said Dunbar. "I sleep with one eye open."

"You know what I mean."

"Sure."

"I've seen all sorts of things, even when you tell people not to."

Dunbar nodded. Hunton turned his glassy eyes on me. I nodded as well. I could tell that here was another person who liked to get in the last word.

Breakfast consisted of flapjacks and molasses with coffee on the side. Hunton made a memorable profile with his nose and his stomach as he stood by the stove with his flapper raised. I tried to imagine him at an earlier age, fighting Indians, and at a subsequent age, courting women.

"No one else came in last night?" asked Dunbar.

"They'd better not."

"No, I meant it as a question. No one else took a room?"

Hunton shook his head. "Just you two." He gave us a critical look where we sat at the table. "Are you passin' through?"

Dunbar said, "We just finished one job, and we're about to go on another. We do ranch work."

"There's plenty of that, this time of year, anyway."

"What do you know about this building project at Stanton's house?"

"I wouldn't count on it. It's his wife's idea. He's not so keen on it. I don't blame him. Some women have no idea of how much things cost."

"We met the fellow who's looking at the work now."

"Sure. They bring 'em in, put 'em up at the Waverly, and send 'em away. I doubt they'll ever put a shovel in the ground."

"Nice enough fellow."

"They all are, when they think there's somethin' in it."

Dunbar said, "The Waverly's a little rich for my blood."

"You're not the only one."

The sidewalk lay partly in shade as we walked toward the livery stable with our bags in hand. With nobody visible within listening distance, Dunbar spoke in a voice not very loud.

"Do you think Holcomb stayed at the Waverly?"

"I don't know. I hadn't thought of him. But I have been thinking about something else."

"What's that?"

"I was wondering what you thought about Mr. Rutledge's plan to build a new town."

"Madeleine? The name is a cordial gesture, almost gallant. A touching memorial to a dead wife." After a couple of seconds, Dunbar continued. "As for the parcels and all that, it sounds like what he said. Speculation. Take away the sweet sentiment, and it seems like what you have is two men selling dirt."

CHAPTER FIVE

The man at the livery stable had an uneven complexion, as if he had had freckles at one time and was given to sunburn. He had light, thin eyebrows and pale blue eyes, and I felt that he saw me as the inexperienced lad that I was. But with Dunbar present, he did not talk down to me.

He had two horses for sale. He brought out the first one on a neck rope, and as soon as the man stopped, the horse hung its head.

"Don't let him fool you," said the man. "He acts like an old plug, but he's got a lot of get-up-and-go."

I nodded as I looked the horse over. It was a heavy-built sorrel, about sixteen hands high. I had heard the men at the ranch say that you could tell at first look whether you liked a horse. I had no feeling at all for this one.

"What do you think? Do you want to get on him?"

"I don't know."

Dunbar said, "Let's see him move."

"You bet." The man led the horse into the stable and came back out with the rope in one hand and a buggy whip in the other. He took the horse into the street, gave it about ten feet of rope, and snapped the whip. The horse began running counterclockwise in a circle as the man turned, whipping the air and making a clucking sound with his mouth. The horse ran with heavy, lumbering steps. After a few revolutions, the man switched hands and ran the horse in the opposite direction.

When he let the horse come to a stop, the animal was breathing hard. It hung its head as before and did not look at the man.

"Let's see the other one," I said.

The stable man put the sorrel away and brought out a smaller, short-coupled horse that was a very dark brown, almost black, with a black mane and tail.

"This fella's got a heart of gold," said the man as he brushed it. "Lotta spirit."

"Is he gentle?" Dunbar asked.

"I wouldn't say he's a kid's horse. But you don't have to be a bronc twister to ride him. Best way to know is to try him yourself."

I said, "Can you have him take a few turns like you did with the other one?"

"Oh, yeah." The man had a halter on the dark horse, with a lead rope about eight feet long. He led the horse into the street and started it in a circle, slapping his pants leg and making the clucking sound. The horse picked up a trot right away, then into a lope, and I liked its smooth motion. The man stopped the horse and started it running clockwise. After a few revolutions, he brought it to a halt. The animal kept its head up and watched the man.

"See what I said? He'd make a good cow pony. But he turns fast. Got quick feet. You gotta look out until you get used to him."

"Will he buck?" I asked.

"I haven't seen him do it, but there's no guarantee on a horse. Like I say, the best way is to try him. Of course, if you're afraid to get on—"

"I'll try him," I said. "Let me get my saddle."

I told myself I couldn't let the horse feel my nervousness, but my hands shook a little as I spread the blankets onto the horse's back, put the saddle in place, and cinched it. The man took off the halter, and I pulled the bridle up over the horse's ears as I settled the bit in his mouth. I walked the horse out a few steps and pulled the cinch one hole tighter.

Here goes, I told myself. I put my foot in the stirrup, held onto the reins and the saddle horn, and pulled myself aboard. As I settled my right leg into place, I felt the horse solid and steady. I held the reins snug until I caught the other stirrup, and then I let the dark horse move forward.

He started out at a walk, first slow and then a little faster. I was conscious of keeping the reins even and my legs not too tight. I began to review what I would do if the horse took off on me, and that was what he did. He broke into a run. I slowed him down, and he resumed his fast walk. I thought I must have telegraphed something to him, maybe a faint twitch of a leg muscle. But he had slowed down when I wanted him to, and he was not skittish.

I turned him around and rode back to the spot where the stable man and Dunbar stood talking.

"What do you think?" said the man.

I knew better than to seem too eager, so I swung down from the horse without answering. I walked around in front with the reins in my hand.

"I could take or leave either one," I said. "How much are you asking for this one?"

"The little bay? Twenty-five."

My stomach sank, and I drew my head back. "I don't have that much. How about the other one?"

"The old sorrel? You could have him for twenty-two."

I shook my head.

"This one's a better kind of horse. That's the difference."

"What's your best price on this dark horse?"

"I gave you a good price."

"Nah. I can't do it." I began to loosen the cinch.

"I'll tell you what. I'll let you have him for the same price as the sorrel. Twenty-two."

I recalled the twenty-three dollars on Rutledge's counter, and I imagined all but one of them disappearing. "Then how much does that make the sorrel worth?"

The man paused and gave me a hard look with his pale blue eyes. "You can have the sorrel for twenty."

My heartbeat had picked up, and I was afraid of doing something I couldn't go back on. But I forged ahead. "If you let me have the dark horse for the same price as the sorrel, I'll take it."

"What do you mean?"

"Twenty." I pulled the latigo and let the cinch fall free.

The corners of his mouth went down. "I can't let you cut my price twice in a row. You can have the sorrel for twenty."

"I don't want him."

"I can't do it."

"Well, I can't spend any more than twenty." I reached across, drew the cinch up, and draped it on the seat. I made ready to pull off the blankets and saddle together.

"All right," said the man. "But I won't get back what I've fed this horse."

I didn't believe him, but I didn't have to answer. Instead, I let him have my four gold pieces before someone else got them.

As we rode out of town, each of us leading a horse, I said to Dunbar, "Do you think I did all right?"

"I didn't know you were such a horse trader."

"I'm not. It was the first time. Did I get a good price, do you think?"

"I'd wait to see if he bucks you off before I decided. For the time being, though, it looks reasonable."

"I was nervous."

"You should have been. The good thing is, you didn't ask me what I would do."

"I almost did."

"It's good you didn't. For one thing, I wouldn't have told you. And for another, it would have ruined your bargaining."

The dark horse stepped along with the other three and gave me no trouble as Dunbar and I rode out into the open country. After what seemed like an endless procession up and down the main street and in and out of businesses, I was glad to be riding across the broad, green grassland under the blue sky. Cattle made dark dots in the distance, while antelope made pale specks. Not having a building in view added to my appreciation. At moments such as this, I could imagine a vast spirit hovering over the land, benevolent but not interfering with hawks tearing apart rabbits, rattlesnakes swallowing prairie dogs, and men devising evil on one another.

On such a calm day on the rangeland, I had the illusion of stability, that sunshine was constant and the prairie was uncomplicated. But in my few months in Wyoming, I had learned that the one thing a person could count on was that the weather would change. By mid- or late afternoon, the skies could darken, bringing wind, rain, and pummeling hail to this land without trees or shelter. I recalled Dunbar's comment to Stanton during that first meeting, that after a time in cold country, a man could remember it on the sunniest day of the year. The same applied to violent summer storms, I thought. Then it occurred to me that it might be an illusion, also, to think of warm, sunny weather as the rule and to consider black clouds or pale blue snow as the exception. Maybe they were balanced, or maybe one was a necessary counterpart to the other, as a preacher in Ohio had said. The jug had two handles. The Old Testament and the New Testament. Sin and salvation.

You couldn't have one without the other.

Once when I was a boy, before my mother left, I spent a wretched day working for an old skinflint whose chicken house and pen had fallen in. The whole place was a mess, with rusty nails sticking up out of boards in a jungle of dead weeds. In the end, when I had it all piled up and the man had paid me twenty-five cents, my mother came for me. The man was pouring coal oil on the lumber and weeds, and I wanted to leave before he lit the fire. At that moment the neighbor lady, who had watched me work all day, came hobbling over on a cane. She was large and overweight, with red hair running to gray.

"Here," she said, giving me a ten-cent piece. "This is for you."

"You don't have to do that," said my mother.

The lady heaved a sigh. "I know. But it's my way of going to heaven."

I often thought of her and why it was a good thing the preacher didn't hear her. He was firm on the idea that people did not get into heaven on good works. They had to recognize that they had sinned, and they had to repent. If it was not fair for God to punish without the promise of redemption, it was also not fair for a person to be saved without asking forgiveness and accepting the Lord. Two handles.

I glanced at Dunbar riding his blue roan and leading the buckskin packhorse. With his tall black hat and his bushy mustache, he reminded me a little of the Old Testament half. His thoughts seemed to be far away, and I wondered if he was thinking of the ice and snow of the frozen north or if his thoughts were a few miles south where a woman named Medora had told us to be sure to come back.

He turned to me and smiled. I was afraid he could read my mind, but he said, "How's the little bay doin' for you?"

"Heart of gold."

"Have you thought of a name for him?"

"Not yet." I nodded toward the palomino. "If that one's Sunny, maybe I should name this one Blackie. Except he's not really black, just the mane and tail."

"Men get nicknamed Blackie when they have black hair. Same with red-haired fellas who get called Red."

"I'll have to think about it," I said.

"Plenty of time."

We rode on for a minute or so until I worked up the courage to ask, "What are your horses' names?"

Dunbar's face was pensive as he said, "I haven't named them yet."

We arrived at Carlyle's when the sun was straight up. The menagerie turned out to greet us with cackles, hisses, and squawks. As before, I kept an eye on the geese as I dismounted.

Carlyle emerged from the house holding the brown hat in his hand and flicking a finger at the furrow that ran down the middle of the crown. "Spiders," he said. He put the hat on his head and surveyed our group. His eyes went up and down on Sunny. "You made it back. Good."

"Thanks for the loan of your horse," I said. "He treated me real well."

"He's a good horse. Just like I said." Carlyle turned to Dunbar. "Any news?"

Dunbar shook his head. "I asked a few people about Ross, but I didn't get anything specific."

"Who-all did you talk to?"

"Jack Brumley, as you suggested. Then an old man named Ambrose Lennox. He suggested I talk to Jane Lancaster, but she didn't want to talk to me."

"That's the midwife. Did she know Ross?"

"Not to speak of, but along the way, I became interested in

the story of Louise Brumley, and I was told that Mrs. Lancaster knew her."

"Might have. That was before I came here."

"I don't know if there's any connection. But it was something that came up, and it caught my attention."

"I still have my doubts," said Carlyle. "About Ross."

"So do I. If we keep our eyes and ears open, something else might come around."

Carlyle squinted as he nodded. "Well, thanks for bringing the horse back." He smiled at me. "Looks as if you got one for yourself."

"I did."

"If you want, you can use that saddle for a while, until you find one of those."

My spirits sank, and I felt like a complete fool. My thoughts had been so absorbed by the horse and other things that I hadn't even thought of a saddle. "Um, well, thanks. I don't know when—"

Dunbar interrupted. "Here was my idea. Neither of us is in a hurry. We thought we could help you out on your place here. Keep an eye on your cattle, and so forth."

Carlyle's eyes opened. "I don't know that I have work for two men. Ross helped out, but he wasn't a full-time hand."

Dunbar held up his hand. "I know what you mean. We're not askin' for pay. Just board and room. We can stay in your barn. Be very little trouble."

Carlyle frowned. "I'm not sure why you'd want to do that."

"First off, we help you out a little. Return the favor for the loan of the horse. And while we're at it, we might pick up something about . . . strange things, you might say."

"I still don't know what your stake in it is."

"I'm curious." Dunbar's glance traveled away and came back. "There was one little bit of news I didn't think of when you asked me a couple of minutes ago."

"And that is—?"

"A new fellow came to town to work for Stanton. At the ranch. He looks more like a gunhand than a cowpuncher. That's one reason I think there might be something else come up."

Carlyle's eyes narrowed. "Are you some kind of a lawman?"

"No. I'm just curious. And I'm not the type to turn my back on something like this until I know more."

Carlyle folded his arms across his chest and took a long breath. "I suppose so. I can always use the help, and there's plenty of room in the barn. As for food, that's one thing we don't run short on. I hope you don't mind boiled cabbage."

"It's like heavenly manna."

Carlyle laughed. "We do have cabbage from time to time, but right now my wife has a good pot of stew on the stove. If you fellas want to unpack in the barn, I'll bring you a couple of bowls."

Dunbar and I rode out that afternoon. I had not seen the country that far east, so I took interest in the rangeland as I kept an eye out for cattle. The grass was sparser here, with patches of alkali, and the bordering hills looked rougher than they did at a distance. We found Carlyle's cattle, split up, and rode around to meet about a half-mile to the north.

"Eleven cows and nine calves," said Dunbar.

"That's what I counted."

"He said he had twenty, so I imagine we found 'em all. Nothing out of the ordinary."

"Not much work," I said.

"Still, we got it done. I suppose we can head back."

Heat rose from the earth as we rode into the afternoon sun. My horse had behaved himself all day, but he began to throw his head every once in a while.

"What do you think is bothering him?" I said. "I don't see a horsefly or anything like that."

Dunbar pursed his lips in a studious expression. "Could be that the headstall has loosened a little, and the bit is slipping in his mouth. Let's see if we can adjust it."

We both dismounted, and I held the reins around the horse's neck while Dunbar took up one notch on the headstall. The horse took the bit again and did not worry it.

Dunbar said, "That's good. See how it tucks in the corner of his mouth and makes him smile? That's what you want."

We mounted up and rode for less than a mile when we saw two riders appear out of a roll in the earth ahead of us. They were heading southwest until one of them turned and looked our way. They stopped and waited.

"Blythe and Slater," I said.

"That's good."

We put our horses into a trot so as not to keep the other two riders waiting long. As I raised in my stirrups, I paid attention to the dark horse and did not give him full rein. I did not want him to run out from under me with the others watching.

We drew up next to Blythe and Slater and exchanged greetings.

"Whose horse?" asked Blythe.

"Mine," I said. "I bought him in town this morning."

"He looks familiar, but I don't remember where I've seen him."

"I got a bill of sale for him."

"Oh, I didn't mean anything. I just thought I'd seen him before."

"What's new at the ranch?" I asked.

Slater said, "Willard got fired."

"He did? What for?"

Slater shook his head. "No tellin'. Kelso told him he was

done, and that was it. You know Kelso. He never liked Willard."

Dunbar spoke in a polite tone. "I wonder why that is. Not that I'm trying to get you to say anything about your foreman, but I wonder why he's had it in for Willard."

Slater did not answer right away. I thought he might be choosing his words to refer to Willard having heard something from Ross Guilford, but all he said was, "That's Kelso. He hates anyone who's not white, and he even hates white people if they're foreigners. So maybe it's for the best. Not for Willard, because he lost his job, but at least there won't be any trouble."

"Huh," said Dunbar. "Did a fella named Holcomb show up?"

"Yes, he did," said Blythe. "We just met him at noon dinner."

"When did Willard leave?" I asked.

"This morning, right after breakfast."

I said, "I hope you get along with Holcomb. Do you think they'll hire anyone else? By my count, they're still one hand short from before."

Blythe said, "I've got no idea." He glanced at Dunbar and back at me. "How about you two? Are you workin' for anyone, just in case anyone asks me what you're doin' out here?"

"We're helpin' out Carlyle," I said.

"Two men for twenty cattle?" Blythe suppressed a smile.

"We dig potatoes, too," said Dunbar.

Blythe laughed. "That's fine with me. I just never know what people see and what they might ask about." He nodded at my horse. "By the way, I remember where I saw that one before. They were selling him at auction."

"Do you remember why?"

"Yep. This fella was stealin' chickens. He climbed aboard with a gunny sack full of 'em, and the horse spooked. Ran under a clothesline and caught the fella by the neck. They buried him and sold the horse to pay the expenses."

"Really?"

79

Slater said, "Don't believe him, kid. He's pullin' your leg."

I looked at Blythe.

"Just funnin' ya. I think I saw that horse in the livery stable."

"That's where I bought him."

"Then I remembered right. I hope he works fine for you." Blythe evened his reins as he made ready to go.

I said, "Thanks. And so long."

"You bet." He and Slater waved, and their horses took off at a walk, tails swishing.

Dunbar sat still and did not speak until the other two rode over a rise and out of sight. After a glance at the sun, he said, "We've got plenty of time. We could stop by Brumley's."

We cut across country to the southwest, through grass that was drier and more sparse than what we had seen already. We rode past a prairie dog town, where the rodents had ruined about twenty acres of pasture land. They sat upright at the mouths of their burrows and watched us until we rode within a hundred yards, and then one by one they dropped into the earth.

"Dirt movers," said Dunbar.

"I've heard they carry vermin."

"So have I. I've never examined one, though. I don't shoot animals for sport, and I've never been so close on food that I had to shoot one for meat. I've heard of men who did. Meat's meat, the old-timers said, especially in the winter, but I've heard these little fellas have a strong taste."

"I don't doubt it."

"I've wondered what their dwellings are like, but I've never dug one up." He gave the town one last look as we rode past it.

Jack Brumley was pumping water into his horse trough when we rode into his yard. He straightened up and turned to greet us. His tired eyes moved over us and our horses.

"What's new?" he asked.

Dunbar shrugged. "Not much."

Brumley's eyes roved again. "People who know me, if they come from town, they bring me a bottle."

"We're learning," said Dunbar.

"You've got a different horse."

I realized he was talking to me. "That's right."

"What did you do with the other one?"

"We took it back to Tom Carlyle."

"Oh, then you didn't just come from town."

"No," I said. "We were out looking at Tom's cattle for him."

Dunbar spoke. "Have you seen Willard?"

"He was by." Jack drew a sack of tobacco from his vest pocket and began to roll a cigarette. He had rough hands with spots on the backs. Without looking up, he said, "They fired him over at Clay Creek. More of Kelso's doin's."

"Sorry to hear that."

Jack held up the cigarette with his thick fingers and licked the edge of the paper. "What do you need him for?"

"We bumped into a couple of Stanton's riders, and they told us Willard had been let go. We weren't far away, so we thought we'd drop in."

Jack raised his eyes. "Then you already knew."

Dunbar's voice had a firm edge on it as he said, "We had been told. We also heard they put on a new hand named Holcomb."

"Never heard of him."

"Well, I hope Willard stays clear of him. We saw Holcomb in town, and he doesn't look like a happy-go-lucky cowhand."

"If he's at the ranch, that's a good place for him. I believe Willard went to town." Jack lit his cigarette. "Thanks for mentioning it."

"A small thing."

Jack already had the end of his cigarette wet. He spit away a fleck of tobacco. "Anything else?"

Dunbar shook his head. "Not really. But I wouldn't mind clarifying one detail from before."

"What's that?"

"Do you think they're picking on Willard because they think he knows something?"

"Like what?"

"Like something Ross Guilford might have said."

"I don't think so. Ross never told anyone anything. So in that sense, there's nothing to know."

"But Kelso or Stanton might think he knows something."

Jack held the cigarette close to his lips. "They might, but I don't know what it would be. They'd be mistaken. As for firing him, they're makin' things difficult for no good reason. But I'll tell Willard to stay clear of 'em."

"That would be a good idea."

"Ideas are like headaches. I don't get 'em very often."

Carlyle brought us beef stew again for supper, along with a tin plate of biscuits. Unlike our recent host Mr. Hunton, he also gave us a small dish of butter. He listened to our brief report as we ate our meal, and when we were done, he took away the dishes and left us to ourselves.

Just as some men had more ideas than others, Dunbar had more patience than I did. He sat on a wooden crate and used an oily cloth to wipe the britching on his packsaddle. He seemed content to be staying in a barn and reducing his affairs to such a simple activity. I felt myself becoming restless, but I sat on my own crate and listened to his talk.

"Back on the subject of eating gophers and prairie dogs, the old-timers used to say they were 'froze for meat.' They'd say, 'We was froze for meat, and I would have et a crow.' Puts me in mind of some men who were really froze."

I had heard the stories about the Donner Party as well as about Alferd Packer, who had lived through the winter on the bodies of some of his companions. I nodded for Dunbar to go on.

"Don't know if you've ever heard of the Franklin Expedition."

"No, I haven't."

"Also called the Lost Expedition. Goes back to the 1840s. Franklin was a captain in the British Navy, and he had made a few Arctic expeditions. In his last one, though, trying to find the Northwest Passage, way north, the group got trapped in ice. They had two ships—with poetic names, *Terror* and *Erebus*—and more than a hundred and twenty men. They all died, some in the first couple of years as they stayed near the ships, and the rest as they set out on foot toward the mainland of Canada."

"Did they freeze to death?"

"Some did, I guess, but there were enough maladies to go around. Scurvy, malnutrition, food poisoning, pneumonia, maybe tuberculosis, and good old-fashioned exposure to the elements."

"And not one survived?"

"None. After they'd been missing for a couple of years, search parties went out. Little by little they found evidence—a few graves, a note left by the group that set out on foot, a few accounts by the natives. Maybe some day they'll have the whole story pieced together. Some parts are still a mystery."

"It sounds like a great disaster."

"It was. Reminds us of the many ways to die in this world. At least in this case, no one died of malice or treachery. Mistakes, maybe, but there's no evidence that anyone lifted a hand against another."

"Would there have been cannibalism?"

"I believe there might have been some of that, from reports. I'm sure it's a last resort in circumstances like that, and the person being eaten has been dead already."

"Meat's meat."

"When you're froze for it."

My restlessness set in again the next morning when Dunbar, still unhurried, went about smearing dark paste on his horses' hooves.

I asked, "Do you have to let that set in for a while?"

"Doesn't hurt. At the very least, I'm in no hurry to go out and stir up a lot of dirt." He let down the buckskin's hoof. "Are you getting anxious to go somewhere?"

"I need to be doing something. I need to make some money so I can buy a saddle."

"Oh. I thought maybe you wanted to go see that girl in the Deville Café."

So he had seen her. "I think not," I said. "I just don't like sitting around not doing anything."

"Neither do I. It's a good reason to stay out of jail." Then, as if he had caught himself being a little too caustic, he took a milder tone. "If you want to take off, go ahead. I'll catch up with you in town in a day or two. Even at that, don't feel as if you're stuck with me."

"It's the other way around. I feel like you're stuck with me and I'm not earning my keep. After all, it takes only one of us to ride out every other day and look at twenty head of cattle."

He tipped his head and tossed a shrug. "It's all right. You're not a burden on anyone, but I understand how you feel. I'll see you later on."

He was being so civil that I almost didn't go, but I felt I had committed myself to it, and I knew I would become impatient again if I sat around. So I led my horse outside, brushed him, and saddled him. As I gathered up my gear, I decided to put my pistol and holster in my saddlebag rather than have it tied down in my duffel bag. When I was rigged and ready to go, I took leave of Dunbar.

"Thanks for your help. I suppose I'll see you later."

"I 'magine." He smiled as he shook my hand. "I hope you have clear sailing."

"Like the *Terror* and the other one, the *Erebus*?"

"Those were steamships. But even they met their match."

Out in the open country, an uneasiness began to gnaw at me as my horse would not settle down. He would skip off at an angle to one side or another, bunch up under me, throw his head, and take off on a beeline. I reined him in every time he acted up, but I was wary of pulling the reins too tight. I had done that once with a ranch horse, and he hunched up and started bucking. I did not want this horse to buck on me. I did not want to have that between us if I could help it.

Onward I rode, with stretches of smooth riding in between the horse's fits and starts. Then he took off on a dead run. I clamped my legs against the saddle, leaned forward, and cheated. I grabbed the saddle horn with my right hand. I held the reins in my left, so I let go of the horn with my right and pulled the slack from my reins. The horse made a sharp left turn, and I went sailing. Clear sailing until I hit the ground.

I landed on my right shoulder and hip, taking quite a jolt. I stood up and tested my leg. My right side from the waist down was tingling, but I could walk. My horse was a hundred yards away, reins dangling as he looked back over his shoulder at me. I began to walk forward, one careful step at a time. The warning from the man at the livery stable came back to me. *He turns fast. You gotta look out until you get used to him.*

I was startled by a different voice.

"Need some help?"

I turned around to see Rich Stanton riding toward me on his red dun. I wondered where he came from, and I assumed he had seen me take a tumble. Still, I said the obvious.

"Horse turned too quick on me."

"He might be hard to catch on foot. Let me go get him for you."

My pride rose up, but common sense took over. "Thanks," I said. I let my weight settle on my left side as I watched Stanton.

He turned his back on me and rode toward my horse. Dressed in his light-colored outfit and jogging along, the man looked harmless. But I wondered if he had been trailing me, and I disliked letting him see me at such poor advantage.

He gathered my horse and came jogging back. He smiled as he handed me the reins with a gloved hand.

"Thanks," I said. "I feel like a fool."

"Don't mention it." He gave the dark horse a onceover. "Not bad-looking."

"I'm just getting used to him."

"Happens to everyone." As he smiled again, I noticed his paling blond hair, his brown eyes, and his face that was filling out with middle age. "You've got the makings of a good rider, though. You'll do all right."

"We'll see, I guess."

"Believe me." His horse shifted, and he tensed his reins. "I told Kelso he shouldn't have fired you. And I meant it. Here, get on your horse. I'll hold the bridle if you want."

"I can do it by myself."

"Sure. Go ahead."

I turned the horse away, snugged the reins, and swung into the saddle.

Stanton spoke again. "I'll ride along with you for a ways."

I did not like his manner at all, but there was nothing I could do. He had helped me with my horse, and he was making polite conversation, but nothing felt right.

"Here's what I think," he said. "That other fellow, Dunbar, got you on Kelso's wrong side. You know how Paul is. As for Dunbar, I don't know him. Maybe you do. But he strikes me as someone who's more likely to hang around than to go to work. As far as I'm concerned, he could move on somewhere else, and no one would miss him. But that's not my concern. What he does is up to him." Stanton paused as he pulled the loose ends of his reins and let them hang free. "Why don't you think about coming back to work for me? Just you, not this other fellow."

I felt a creeping sensation, as if Stanton had put his arm across my shoulders and was about to settle his hand on the back of my neck. I had an awareness of my gun being out of reach, and I didn't know if I could use it even if I had it in my hand.

"Maybe you don't want to work at the ranch, and I wouldn't blame you. But the things that were eating on Paul have gone away. I think he'll sweeten up. Still, I've got other work. I think my father-in-law mentioned Madeleine to you."

My idea of Madeleine was that she was in her grave. I was impressed by Stanton's referring to the place as if it already existed. Trying to play in as little as possible, I said, "The town."

"That's it. As I imagine Gilbert told you, we'll need someone to keep an eye on things, once the project gets under way."

"Uh-huh."

"You could work on your own, not have someone breathing down your neck."

The prickly feeling crept through me again.

"Think about it, Whit. I don't know where you're headed right now. Looks like you're on your way to town. But if you wanted, you could—"

Hoofbeats behind us signaled a horse at a gallop. Stanton and I stopped our horses and turned back to look.

Dunbar was riding our way on the blue roan. Fifty yards out, he slowed his horse and came in at a walk.

"Good day," he said. "Almost afternoon."

"Same to you," said Stanton.

"Fair weather for a ride," Dunbar continued.

"Indeed."

"My young friend took off ahead of me. I told him I'd catch up so he didn't have to ride alone. Didn't expect him to have company, but it's always welcome."

Stanton mumbled something that sounded like "Yep." I thought he might have felt embarrassed for having spoken light of Dunbar just a minute before, but Stanton's demeanor suggested to me that he wanted to avoid any direct confrontation with Dunbar. He had an open opportunity to talk about the town project, the weather, or anything else, as men so often did to shade out something they had said a few minutes earlier. But Stanton did not.

Dunbar said, "By the way, your father-in-law mentioned an opportunity to help out in a project you're planning."

"Oh, yes," said Stanton.

"We haven't forgotten about it. That's for sure."

"Good." Stanton brought the red dun to a stop. "This is where I turn."

"You're welcome to ride along with us," said Dunbar.

"Thanks, but I need to go this way." Stanton touched his cream-colored hat. "See you later."

"Always a pleasure."

Dunbar and I rode on. When Stanton and the red dun were half a mile away, Dunbar said, "Where did he come from?"

"I don't know. I got tossed from my horse, and when I looked up, there he was." I gave Dunbar a sideways look. "And yourself?

I didn't expect to see you so soon."

"I got restless, too. Must be contagious. Or maybe it was just the thought of apple pie." After a couple of seconds, he added, "I hope I didn't interrupt your conversation."

I reflected on Stanton's cheap comments about Dunbar and then his apparent wish to avoid him. I said, "Not at all. I was glad to see you show up."

CHAPTER SIX

The Deville Café showed signs of having passed through the midday dinner hour. Two men sat lingering over coffee at a window table while several other tables had dishes stacked and ready to be cleared away. Medora met us in the middle of the dining area, her face glowing with exertion and a hint of perspiration.

"Good afternoon," she said with a smile. "I see you came back."

Dunbar took off his hat. "As fast as the horses would gallop."

Her dark eyes sparkled. "Really?"

"Almost."

She turned to her left. "Here's a clean table by the wall. Please have a seat."

I took off my hat as well, and the two of us pulled out chairs.

The girl I had seen two days before appeared from the kitchen. Like Medora, she had dark hair and wore a white blouse and a black skirt. Her hair was straighter than Medora's and longer, falling past her shoulders, and her skin had a deeper complexion. As they passed next to each other, I saw that the girl had a tinge of bronze. Her figure was not as full as Medora's, but it was shapely. I guessed her to be about a year younger than myself. My pulse quickened when her dark eyes met mine for a second and she did not look away.

"Here, Eva," said Medora. "Clear this table next."

The girl set a tray on the table next to us and turned to her

90

work. As she moved, I caught the sight of her rich, dark hair cascading across her shoulders. I made myself look away so that I would not be caught gaping.

Medora stood by our table with a hand on her hip. With a very slight notion she straightened her shoulders. "Are you interested in a meal, or something less?"

Dunbar's eyes left her, and he frowned. I followed his line of sight and saw the cause of his distraction. Ambrose Lennox was looking in through the glass pane of the door and making urgent hand gestures.

"Excuse me," said Dunbar. He rose from his chair and took calm steps toward the door. The two men at the window watched him as he stepped outside and closed the door behind him.

I looked at Medora and gave a polite smile.

"I'll be back," she said.

The girl named Eva lifted the tray of dishes from the nearby table. She smiled to me as she turned, and I almost swooned, though I summoned up a smile. I was filled with a rush of wonder as her presence seemed to glow out from her, but Dunbar's voice brought me back.

"I think we'd better go. Willard Brumley has gone on a tear, and he's likely to get into trouble. Lennox said he went to the Waverly Hotel and gave a string of abuse to Mr. Rutledge."

Dunbar remained standing as he gathered up his hat. I rose from my chair and laid my hand on my hat.

Medora returned and said, "Are you leaving?"

"Something came up," said Dunbar. "We'll be back."

"I hope it's not too serious."

"No telling. It's good to see you, though, and we'll be back when we can do honor to some apple pie. Or whatever is in the pantry by then."

Medora smiled. "We'll be here."

I looked around for Eva, but I did not see her. I said goodbye to Medora and followed Dunbar out the door.

"Let's go on foot," he said.

We set out in the calm afternoon. The sun was shining in a clear sky, and only a faint breeze stirred. No one appeared on the street. A few horses were tied to hitching rails, but no wagons or even carts showed signs of activity.

Dunbar said, "I don't know how bad this is. Lennox may have been overstating things. But it's been a full day since Willard was fired, so he has had time to get worked up."

We did not slow down as we passed the Dakota Rose. We went straight to the Waverly Hotel and up the steps.

Gilbert Rutledge met us at the door. He was wearing a bluish-gray suit and was as well groomed as always, but he had an air of agitation about him. He said, "I was on my way out, but come in. What do you need?"

Dunbar said, "We were in town but a few minutes when we heard that Willard Brumley had been down here causing a disturbance."

An expression of annoyance crossed Rutledge's face. "What are you, some kind of a constable?"

"No, but if I can help keep him out of trouble—"

"Oh, that worthless kid."

"He's hardly a kid. He's at least twenty-five years old."

"He doesn't act like it. He's a bastard to begin with, and he acts like a ruffian. What you'd expect from a mulatto."

Dunbar's eyes opened wide. "Well, now. It sounds like you've been talking to Kelso."

"I don't have much to do with him."

"Neither do I, but that's the way he talks, and I think a great deal of the trouble has been provoked by him."

"Maybe so, but he doesn't come around acting uncouth like that Brumley kid does."

"How many times has Willard been here?"

"Once. And that was enough."

"I imagine he came to draw his pay."

"He did, and I paid him. I hope it's good riddance."

"I doubt that he'll be back," said Dunbar.

"He'd better not. I won't be spoken to that way again."

"If all he did was talk, I would say, rise above it."

"He all but spit in my face. Liquor on his breath." Rutledge's nostrils widened.

"I'm not defending him, but maybe he has reason to be on a rampage. Something touched him off."

"I would say so. But he must have a low boiling point."

"Maybe he's touchy, but you know, the boy hasn't had it easy."

"See? You're calling him a boy yourself."

Dunbar said with a deliberate tone, "I was referring to his upbringing. The boy grew up without a mother."

"Oh, that."

"It can't be easy, growing up with the idea that your mother left you."

Rutledge shrugged. "I don't know what you can expect from some people anyway."

Dunbar's face tensed, but the tone of his voice remained measured. "I understand that you're one of the more knowledgeable people in town, and I imagine you were here at the time that his mother went away."

"Oh, yes. That was back in the time when Madeleine was alive and Richard was courting Agnes. About twenty years ago."

"Then you would remember Louise Brumley."

"Somewhat."

"And she just disappeared?"

"Packed up and left."

"Did she pack up?"

"My God, Mr. Dunbar, I have no idea. I was not that interested. As far as I know, not that many people were sad to see her go. She was just a mulatto anyway."

"Well, she was the boy's mother. That's what I was getting at."

"I know, I know."

"I guess I have a little sympathy for him, and I'd like to see him stay out of trouble. And as far as that goes, I'd better get to looking for him."

"Good luck, and I hope you find him before he gets into something worse. Not everyone will be as tolerant as I am."

We walked out of the hotel and down the front steps with petunias blooming on either side. As we stood on the sidewalk, I could see the town well and Rich Stanton's house a little more than a block away.

"There he is," said Dunbar.

Glancing to my left, I saw Willard Brumley storming into the Dakota Rose saloon.

We lost no time following him, and as the door was open, we walked in without ceremony. Willard stood at the bar, and Ambrose Lennox sat at his usual table. They were the only patrons in the bar other than Dunbar and myself.

"Come over here and sit down," said the old man.

Dunbar and I hesitated. Willard glanced at Lennox and turned toward us.

His tan face was flushed, his eyes were bloodshot, and he had a wild look to him. I could understand why Rutledge had been agitated.

Dunbar said, "Hello, Willard."

"Afternoon."

"Care to join us at the table with Mr. Lennox?"

"Not really."

"Sorry to hear they let you go at the ranch."

Willard had the corners of his mouth turned down. "Don't feel sorry for me. It was going to happen sooner or later. So I say, up their ass."

Lennox's voice floated thin across the empty space. "What did they fire you for, Willard?"

"They didn't give me a reason. I s'pose they don't need one."

"Yeah, that's them. Well, come over here, boys, and don't make me sit alone."

Willard leaned an elbow on the bar. "I'll stay here."

Dunbar and I moved to the table and sat down. I did not like the feeling in the air. I could see that Willard was on a drunk and was primed for a fight. Dunbar acted nonchalant, but he kept an eye on the door and on Willard.

Lennox began talking in a loud voice, as if for everybody's benefit, though he addressed the first part of his speech to me. "I heard you bought a horse. I tell you, it's not the way it used to be. When I worked for Elliot, back when he had the stable, you could have your pick of half a dozen. He could tell you the whole story on any one of 'em—who owned the horse before, what he used it for, any trouble they ever had with it. With this fella that's got the place now, it's like buyin' a pig in a poke. You don't know where the horses came from, and you can't believe what he says about how old they are. Me, I can tell a horse's age within a year or two. One time a fella tried to sell Elliot a horse and said it was fifteen years old. I said, 'Jack, that horse is twenty if he's a day.' Turns out I was right. That horse went from one man to another over a period of five years, and every one of 'em said he was fifteen. So that horse was fifteen for a long time, until I told Jack what I thought, and he checked up on it. He'd already bought it by the time he found out, but after that, he didn't try to sell it for anything other than its true age. And when I say Jack, I mean Elliot, of course. Not your old man."

Willard said, "Oh, dry up."

"I'm tellin' the truth."

"That doesn't make it any more interesting."

"To me it does. That's the trouble nowadays. People don't care about what's the truth and what isn't. Time was, a man—"

"Ah, go on. There's always been liars."

"If you say so. Hah. That reminds me of a riddle. Suppose a man comes up to you and says, 'I've got a thousand dollars to give away, but I won't give it to you if you tell the truth. Do you want it?' Now, what would you say?"

Willard made a spitting sound. "I'd tell him I didn't think he had the thousand dollars."

"Then you wouldn't answer him. He wouldn't give it to you."

"Oh, give up. He wouldn't anyway."

Light flickered in the doorway as two men walked in. My heart jumped and my throat tightened as I saw who they were. Kelso and Holcomb.

Willard turned away to give them the shoulder.

Kelso rapped on the bar with the edge of a silver dollar. "Well, if it ain't the boys' club here."

I wondered if he would be so brave without Holcomb at his side. Holcomb, in turn, stood in his hunched way with his beak nose prominent, and he made his presence more significant by not saying anything.

"Give us a bottle," said Kelso to the bartender. "That way we can share it."

Dunbar and I had not yet ordered drinks, but Lennox and Willard each had a glass of whiskey.

The bartender set a bottle and two glasses on the bar in front of Kelso and Holcomb.

Kelso said, "Pour one for each of us, and then pour one for each of our friends."

"I don't care to drink right now," said Dunbar.

I said, "Neither do I."

Lennox's voice was creaky as he said, "I've got plenty."

Willard spoke over his shoulder. "I'm no friend of yours."

"Be that as it may," said Kelso. "Pour two, and it won't go to waste."

The bartender poured three fingers of whiskey into each of the two glasses.

Kelso took a sip and said, "Aahh. That's wot we came for."

Dunbar kept his eye on the two men. I could see that Kelso made an effort to ignore him.

"This is the best part of my work," said Kelso. When no one responded, he said, "Hirin' a new man."

I couldn't help looking at Holcomb, as the others did.

Kelso made a casual turn to his left, where Holcomb stood. "Not him. He's been around for a couple of days." Kelso took another sip. "It's hard to find a good hand. Hired men want to give you sass about one thing or another. So you've got to go through a few men till you get the right crew." Kelso turned to Holcomb again. "Tell that kid to come in."

Holcomb walked to the door, stood hunched with his thumbs on his gunbelt, and made a shrill whistling sound. He motioned with his head, then walked back to the bar.

Half a minute later, a gangling young man about my age, dressed in a cowpuncher outfit, appeared at the doorway and ventured forward.

Kelso turned and said, "Leave the horses tied up, and go down to the Waverly Hotel. Get yourself something to eat. Tell 'em you're with us. We'll be along in a little while."

"Leave the horses here?"

"That's right. Make sure they're tied and go eat."

"You bet." The kid walked out, followed by his shadow.

I let out a slow breath. I had known Kelso for a few months, yet I was appalled by the way he bossed around and showed off his new hired hand. And he was not done. As if to rub it in, he said, "I imagine you wonder why you got fired, Willard."

"I don't care."

"You ought to. You just don't want anyone to say it in front of your friends here."

"They're not my friends."

"They stick up for you, or they did."

"You called 'em your friends a few minutes ago."

"Maybe I did."

"Well, a friend of yours is no friend of mine."

"Does that go for Mr. Holcomb here?"

My heartbeat jumped again and did not go down.

Willard said, "Leave me alone."

"I'll tell you whether you want to hear it or not." Kelso moved half a step back from the bar and stood with his arms free. His upper lip area was tight over his teeth. "And here it is. A cow outfit has got no room for thieves."

"What?"

Kelso's voice came out slow. "You know wot I'm talkin' about. A jewel case from one of the rooms of the ranch house. A jewel case belongin' to one of the members of the boss's family."

"You don't make any sense."

"I guess I do. A personal belongin' of a person whose name doesn't get spoken in a place like this."

If I was appalled before, I was amazed now by Kelso's false delicacy, in itself a small feature in comparison with the largeness of the accusation.

Willard's voice was firm and clear, not slurred as I thought I had heard it earlier. "I didn't do any such thing."

Kelso's lip remained tight. "A person who'll steal will also lie." After a pause he said, "You've got it in your blood to do low things."

Dunbar rose halfway from his chair, and Kelso held his tongue.

Silence hung in the air for a long moment after Dunbar sat down. I felt a buzzing or humming sensation in my head, as if I was detached from myself and the scene around me. Things didn't make sense. I had never been an admirer of Willard's, but I did not think he would go into the ranch house and take something that belonged to Mrs. Stanton or one of the girls. I found Kelso's manner repugnant and, furthermore, I felt a great fear that he was not going to have to answer for it.

I watched Willard. I had seen men in his condition before— drunk but startled into a state of clear thinking. He had moved away from the bar, and now he was cautious. He looked back and forth from Kelso to Holcomb. He could see himself outnumbered two to one, by men with their guns slung and ready. He was wearing a gun, also, but the odds were unquestionable.

Kelso spoke again. "That's what it was. Theft."

"I didn't do it."

Kelso raised his chin. "Are you calling me a liar?"

"I'm saying I didn't do anything of the sort."

Now Holcomb joined in. "Like Kelso said, it's in your blood to do something low like that."

Each time they mentioned blood, a feeling of dread flowed through me. I knew they were pushing to a bad end.

Kelso moved another step away from the bar, leaving a clear line of fire between Holcomb and Willard. My heart was pounding, and my mouth was dry. I was glad to see Willard keeping himself under control. He had heard it once already, and I thought he could go through it again.

Holcomb continued. "Lie and steal. You've got it in your blood to do that. In your dirty, half-breed blood."

Willard's chest went up and down, but he did not make a

move for his gun. Dunbar stood up, and Willard waved him off.

"I don't need anyone else fightin' my fights for me. I'll stand here and take what these egg-suckers have to say."

Holcomb took the lead. "That's brave of you. I wonder where you get that kind of courage."

"Not from the bottle, like some of you."

"Maybe you get it from the same place you get that dark skin."

I could see Willard's lower lip and jaw begin to tremble. I began to fear for him—for what he might hear, and for what he might do. And I did not feel that this was happening to him alone. I felt part of it, though I could see that he felt all by himself.

Holcomb's voice slowed down as he said, "Your dark skin. Did you get it from your mother, or did you get it from someone else?"

Willard was lost. He had been pushed too far, and I could see it. He was all alone against something he couldn't push back.

Holcomb said, "Was it someone from the woodpile?"

Willard clawed for his gun, and Holcomb beat him. The blast filled the saloon, rocking the overhead lamp and blowing out the flame. Willard doubled over and fell on his side, with his gun still in his holster. A seam of blood appeared at his mouth.

A wave of bewilderment washed over me. I had seen a man killed in front of me. It was not something detached, like an old man lying under the open sky. It was something close and familiar, and it could have happened to me.

Dunbar was standing, facing Kelso and Holcomb.

Kelso tucked in his chin and said, "No need to make things worse. You seen it for yourself. Willard had been drinkin', and he tried to pull a gun on this man."

CHAPTER SEVEN

Dunbar and I sat with Willard's body in the back room of the Dakota Rose while a messenger took the news to Jack Brumley. We didn't have much to say. Dunbar's detached, almost droll, view of the many ways by which people could come to grief, as in the story of the Franklin Expedition, seemed far away. The bodies of a hundred and twenty men, scattered across the frozen wastes of Canada, figured small in comparison with the still, dark body of a man who had raged in defiance not an hour earlier.

After a long silence, though I couldn't have said how long, Dunbar spoke.

"I should have done something anyway. But they surprised me, both of them. I didn't think Holcomb would take it that far—or rather, I didn't know there was that place they could take it. Willard surprised me, too, because he had just said he was going to let them talk. And yet I shouldn't have been surprised by any of it. I'm no stranger to the lowness of men."

"You don't mean Willard was low, do you?"

"Oh, no. I meant the other two. I think Willard weakened, or lost his control, all in that last second. That was his undoing."

I thought so, too, but I couldn't put words to it at that moment—how Willard, alone, gave in, as if he had had some sense of fate or destiny and time had come for him. He couldn't have thought it through, not at the end. He just acted, as Dunbar said, all in that last second.

Dunbar continued. "I don't think he did what they accused him of. I doubt that any jewel case went missing."

"But why would they drum it up? Just because he was colored?"

Dunbar shook his head. "I don't think that was the main reason. I think his being dark helped them, or made it easy for them, to push him into a fight. But as I've suggested before, I think they thought he knew something. His father said he didn't."

I recalled Dunbar's earlier comment, with regard to Ross Guilford, that people died for knowing things. I said, "Do you think he did?"

"I'm inclined to believe his father, but I don't rule out possibilities without a good reason."

"There must be something to be known."

Dunbar shrugged. "That doesn't mean he knew it, even if they thought he did."

"What would it be?"

He pushed out his mustache and relaxed it. "I don't like to say too much too soon. Call me superstitious. But I don't like to hamstring my own efforts."

I gave him a close look. "Are you working for somebody?"

"I work on my own. When I follow my curiosity."

"I thought you might be some kind of a detective."

"I'm a cowpuncher. But sometimes I follow my curiosity, like other people go out and collect butterflies."

I imagined Dunbar, in his tall black hat and dark mustache, frolicking in a flowery meadow and waving a butterfly net. Then I came back to the moment, the two of us sitting with Willard's still, silent body in the back room of a saloon. I felt guilty for being frivolous, yet I knew Dunbar had just taken a light touch as well. And it didn't seem to compromise his larger purpose.

★ ★ ★ ★ ★

Jack Brumley came to town dressed in his everyday work clothes. He had ridden in right away. His face had a somber cast to it, accentuated by the dark bags under his eyes. He did not speak as he stood by his son's body and then knelt.

After a few minutes, he stood up and spoke to Dunbar. "You were there at the time?"

"Yes, I was. I wish I could have done something, but they pushed him too far, all in an instant, and it was over."

"It's what they wanted."

"If there's anything we can do now, like ride back to the ranch with you, or go for the preacher—"

"Just leave me alone with my son."

Night was falling as we walked to the Deville Café. We had left after the dinner hour, and now we were returning after supper. I was hungry, and I hoped Medora would have some good provisions on hand, but I still felt guilty about showing normal feelings in the wake of what had happened to Willard.

As the jingle of the doorbell faded, the interior of the café brightened my outlook. Lamplight was shining, and the aroma of cooked meat hovered in the air. The tables were cleared, the chairs were all straightened up, and Medora stood at the counter jotting figures on a sheet of paper. She set down her pencil and touched her hair.

"I'm glad to see you back. I heard about what happened. It sounds terrible. And nothing happened to the man who did it?"

Dunbar shook his head. "He's got an excuse, with no one to contradict him."

"I know the young man who died, Willard Brumley. He came in here once in a while. Quiet and moody, kept to himself, but hardly the type to deserve something like that."

"They had it in for him."

Medora frowned. "I don't know the one who they say did the shooting. I know the other one, Kelso. I'm not sure what I would have expected of him, probably nothing pleasant, but this is, I don't know, very upsetting. Demoralizing. People shouldn't do things like that in a civilized place. And then to say that they have a justification."

"I know," said Dunbar.

"I'm sorry. You came in here to eat, not to listen to me. At least I assume you'd like something to eat. Am I correct?"

"Quite so. In what you said as well as in your assumption. We were hoping you hadn't closed the kitchen."

"There's still some stew in the pot. That was the main menu this evening, by the way."

Dunbar looked at me. "Shall we?"

"I should say so."

We each put away a large bowl of stew and a half-dozen cold biscuits in about ten minutes. I was beginning to think about the prospect of apple pie when Dunbar spoke to Medora, some ten feet away.

"What time is it getting to be?"

She turned and looked at a clock on the shelf behind the counter. "It's almost nine o'clock." She gave a small gasp. "Oh, my. I was supposed to go to the butcher's. We're out of bacon for the morning." She looked at our dishes and again at the clock. "I know I can go to the back door. I've done it before. I suppose you want pie. Do you?"

"It was in our thoughts, but we can wait."

"No, I'll send Eva. She can go, and I'll tend to you." Medora raised her voice and called, "Eva." Back to us, she said, "I forgot all about it. Too much distraction. This thing that happened earlier."

Eva presented herself, dressed in white and black as I had seen her before.

"Here, Eva," said Medora. "I forgot to go for bacon. I'd like you to go to the butcher's. You can go to the back door. It's all right. I've done it before, you know. Bring ten pounds if he has it. Or five at least, I hope. He'll put it on my bill."

Eva kept her eyes on Medora and said nothing.

"Excuse me," said Dunbar. "I hope you don't mind my interference, but I think it's a bit late to be sending a girl by herself. Not trying to scare anyone. But going to the back door, and all. One of us could help."

Medora said, "Oh, no. You're in the middle of your meal. You've barely had a chance to sit down after everything else, and it's late for you just as it is for me." She held her hand as if to keep Dunbar in his seat.

Dunbar smiled, and his eyes had a shine. "What I meant was, Whit can go with her." He turned to me. "Can't you?"

I was taken off guard. "Well, I guess I can." I saw Medora and Eva both looking at me. "Of course I can. There's nothing to worry about but the dark."

Medora turned to Eva. "Do you mind?"

"No. I can go."

"Good. Get a bag from the kitchen, but go out the front door. Stay on the sidewalk there and back."

Eva nodded.

My mind was swirling, but a minute later I was out in the starry night with Eva. I had taken to wearing my gun most of the time now, and though I felt she might think I was a show-off, I also thought it might give her a sense of being protected.

Eva walked next to me carrying a canvas shopping bag. She did not speak, so I felt I had to say something.

"So your name's Eva."

"Yes, it is. Short for Evangeline."

"That's a pretty name. It's French, isn't it, originally?"

"Yes."

"Medora's last name is French, too, I believe."

"So is mine."

"Oh?"

"Beaulieu."

"Are your parents French, then? I would guess at least one of them is."

"My father is. He's more French than Indian. And my mother is more Indian than French. That's what they always say."

"And where are they?"

"They're here. My father works in the kitchen. My mother takes care of Medora's house and helps at the café. His name is Henry. Her name is Priscilla. Originally it was Sarcelle, for the duck that they call the teal, but where everyone speaks English, it turned into Priscilla."

She said it all in a breath, it seemed, and I didn't want her to stop talking. I said, "I didn't know your parents lived here. I don't know that I've ever seen them."

"Mmm-hmm."

"Have they known Medora for a while?"

"My father used to work for Medora's father, Mr. Bordulac. We came here from the north country to work for Medora."

"The north country. Canada?"

"No, Montana. Choteau, if you know it."

"I don't. I'm from Ohio, myself. But I'd like to see other places."

"They're pretty. We have cousins in Grand Forks. It's a long ways away, in Dakota. We went there once."

"And Medora's father's name, is it French, too?"

"Bordulac? Yes, it is. It means the edge of the lake."

"And your own last name?"

"Beaulieu? It means handsome place, or pretty place."

"That's nice."

We arrived at the butcher's back door. He had us wait there

until he returned with a slab of bacon wrapped in newspaper. We settled it into the shopping bag, like a pig in a poke, and I carried it. I guessed the weight at ten pounds.

As we started back to the café, I asked, "Do you have any brothers or sisters?"

"Not that are alive."

"I'm sorry."

"It's all right."

I could not think of any other suitable questions to ask her, and she didn't volunteer more information about herself. Nor did she ask me about myself. I hoped she was as nervous and uncertain as I was, and not uninterested.

When we reached the café, I said, "Well, here we are."

"Thank you for going with me," she said.

I had the presence of mind to say, "Thank you for going with me."

She lowered her eyelids and smiled. "You're welcome."

Inside the café, Medora and Dunbar were seated across the table from each other. They were both relaxed and had a cordial air about them. For the first time, it occurred to me that Dunbar's move of sending me along with Eva was not limited to her interest and mine.

Medora stood up and said, "I'm glad to see you made it without any trouble. Thank you."

"A pleasure," I said.

Her face had good color as she smiled. "And now for the apple pie. A treat well earned."

We took a room again at Hunton's lodging house. As he gave Dunbar the key, he said we could have the same room.

"Same rules, too. No smoking and no guests. By the way, did you hear about the shootin'? I guess someone got killed in the Dakota Rose."

"We were close by at the time," said Dunbar.

"Too bad about things like that. The fella who got killed was from here. I guess bad luck runs in that family."

Dunbar showed no sign of being in a hurry. "Did you know the family back then, when the boy's mother left?"

"No, I came later. But I know they didn't take it well. Too bad about some women. Not satisfied with what they got." He reached into his vest pocket and took out a toothpick. "Some men, too." He poked the toothpick into his molars. "I guess the fella who came out on top was pretty fast. Was that right?"

"Right in what way?"

"What I mean is, is it true that he was fast?"

"I'm no judge of those things," said Dunbar.

"Well, I hope he's not trying to build a reputation around here. We don't need it." When Dunbar didn't answer, Hunton said, "Breakfast is at the same time as before."

Dunbar said, "We'll look forward to it."

In our room, Dunbar hung his hat on a hook and stretched out on his cot. I sat on the edge of mine.

He said, "I hope you had a nice visit with your girl."

"I wouldn't call her my girl. I barely met her."

"I'm sure you got to know her a little bit. Is she related to Medora?"

"She and her parents work for Medora. Her father works in the kitchen."

"Oh. That's who the man was."

"The one you referred to last time. I didn't see him."

"No matter. Just for the sake of information, what's their last name?"

"Beaulieu. Her full name is Evangeline Beaulieu."

"Evangeline. That's the name of Longfellow's poem about the separated lovers. They were Acadians, you know, like I mentioned the other day at Brumley's. The sweethearts got separated when the people were all moved out of Canada. Good story, full of sorrow."

I said, "I know. I've read it."

"I should have thought of that. I suppose you've read *Uncle Tom's Cabin* as well. There's a girl named Eva there. Short for Evangeline."

"Yes, but I didn't want to be the one to mention it. I'm like you. Superstitious."

We were saddling our horses in the livery stable the next morning when Ambrose Lennox presented himself. He stood by, poking his cheek out with his tongue, until the stable man went out back to the corrals.

"Glad to see you haven't left town yet," said Lennox.

Dunbar lifted a stirrup and hooked it on the saddle horn as he prepared to run the latigo through the cinch ring. He said, "It's hard to tell how much good I do when I'm here."

"I could say the same for myself, and I never leave. I guess Jack took the body with him, to bury Willard at the ranch."

"I guess."

"No surprise that the story's made its way around town."

Dunbar pulled on the cinch strap. "I doubt that very many people care all that much. About who it happened to, that is."

Lennox gave a long sniff. "Willard wasn't the kind of fella who would go around causin' people to like him. Still, not everyone likes to see things set up that way, 'specially when they know it was carried over from somethin' earlier."

"Referring to—?"

"Referring to the little incident that caused Kelso to fire you and the kid here." Lennox turned his jaundiced brown eyes my way and gave me a brief smile.

"I don't know that that's the extent of it."

"Maybe it isn't. But that's what people seem to think they

know. Kelso was pickin' on Willard, you stuck up for him, Kelso fired you two, then he fired Willard, and then him and Holcomb the Hawk pushed Willard into a fight."

"If Mr. Rutledge were telling the story, he would include Willard going on a rampage."

"Could be, but the point I'm gettin' around to is that some people appreciate what you've done." Lennox cast a glance in the direction of the corrals where the stable man had gone. "Point is that Jane Lancaster says she might talk to you after all."

"Did she tell you this individually?"

"Yes. On the *q.t.,* you might say."

"Uh-huh." Dunbar was giving Lennox more serious consideration now. "Do you think she would be interested in talking to me before we left town today? That is to say, was she that definite, or was it a more general inclination?"

"I would say she was that definite."

"Very well. Thanks." Dunbar took off his glove, reached into his pocket, and took out a coin I did not see well. He slipped it into Lennox's hand.

A tinge of pride crept into the old man's ravaged face. "Thank you, sir. You didn't have to do that. It wasn't my motive."

Dunbar smiled. "It wasn't mine, either."

Dunbar and I walked to Mrs. Lancaster's house as the cool of the morning lingered in the air. I had thought we would ride, but Dunbar said it would be better to leave the horses at the stable. I imagined that he did not want to have me and the horses in plain view outside the house while he was inside. He seemed more cautious than before, but he was also direct. He did not need any reminding from me to find the woman's house.

Mrs. Lancaster's residence was a small, one-story wooden structure with weathered gray paint. The two front windows, one on each side of the door, had the blinds drawn, and the door was solid without a pane of glass. We stood on the wooden steps as Dunbar knocked on the door casing.

The door opened, and Jane Lancaster appeared, looking very much as always. She was slender, not very tall, wearing a gray dress and a white apron. Her short, gray hair framed her face, pale in complexion with a dull red nose in the center. Her mouth was set firm as her brown eyes roved over Dunbar and me.

"Mr. Dunbar," she said.

He took off his hat. "Good morning, Mrs. Lancaster. This is Whit Barnett. I hope you don't mind his coming along. He's trustworthy."

I took off my hat and offered a faint smile. I felt conscious of wearing my gun.

Her gaze passed over me again, and she paid no attention to my six-gun. "I hope so. What I have to say is rather confidential."

"I understand." Dunbar smiled as if to charm her into his confidence, but he knew when to stop. He said, "It's not the same as a secret, though. A secret is best kept by one person. After that, some information is better held by more than two people—sometimes for verification, so that no one can say I made up what I may claim that I heard, or for continuity, so that, in a situation I don't like to imagine, the information would not die even if I happened to do so." He shrugged. "All philosophical, of course."

"Please come in." She stood aside.

We walked into her sitting room, a dim area with a small couch and two cushioned chairs with padded arm rests and wooden legs. She sat on the couch, and we sat in the chairs.

She did not speak right away, so Dunbar took the initiative.

"Ambrose Lennox said you might be willing to visit with me. I imagine it has something to do with recent events."

She closed her eyes and gave a slow nod of her head. "Some recent, and some, perhaps not so recent."

Dunbar waited for her to continue.

"Ambrose tells me that Richard Stanton's men had said ugly things about Willard and about his mother."

"I've been present when they've said such things."

"He also tells me that you took up their cause in an earlier situation."

"It was something of a matter of principle, as I had not known Willard for long and of course had never met his mother."

"Well, I was glad to hear you took up for them."

"I wish I could have done more. I feel as if I should have. Especially when they goaded Willard into a fight. I was there, and I should have been able to do something."

"Ambrose said they wouldn't give up. They kept pushing."

"That's true."

"And Willard was not on good behavior, prior to that."

"So I've heard."

Mrs. Lancaster took a long, slow breath. "Even if he didn't conduct himself well, then or before, I always felt sorry for him, and I don't think he deserved to be pushed into that kind of a situation, where he had no way out. From what I understand, it was intended to end that way."

Dunbar's eyes held steady. "I have no doubt about that."

"I don't think he was ever treated fair. The same with his mother." She paused, as if she was getting her words in order, and the silence in the room seemed to nudge her forward. "Maybe Louise wasn't perfect, but she was human like anyone else."

She paused again. Dunbar nodded, and I did the same.

"Everyone said she ran away. That was the common opinion, their judgment on a woman who was bad. Her husband felt she had run off on him, and her son felt abandoned."

I felt a sting of discomfort and waited for her to say something more.

"I thought as others did, that she had run away. I thought she did it because she had become close to another man and had become expectant by him."

Dunbar spoke in a calm voice. "This last part is new. I haven't heard it anywhere else."

"It's my belief. I might have had conversations with her that no one else did."

Dunbar nodded in agreement.

"The common view was that she had run off with someone who came through from time to time. She was reported to have been seen in North Platte in the company of a man who had been seen here in this town."

"Interesting," said Dunbar.

"Yes, but as time has gone by, I have not always thought the way I did back then."

"You say, 'not always.'"

"True. I've had different ideas about the matter. Sometimes I wonder if she went away on her own free will, and sometimes I wonder if she even went away."

"There is quite a range of possibilities," said Dunbar.

"Yes, and I think it will be very hard to know for sure. But, until we do, I don't believe people should be so harsh on her. Like I said, she was human. We all have our flaws." Her cautious brown eyes moved to me and back to Dunbar. "I am not much of a believer, but I agree with the part about being the first to cast a stone."

Dunbar said, "So do I."

"Anyway," said Mrs. Lancaster, with a tone of having said enough if not too much, "I am sorry for all the sadness that has fallen on that family. We learn to live with old sorrows, but this new one is terrible. I am very sorry for it."

Dunbar nodded again. He said, "We're planning to go out that way, to lend a hand to Tom Carlyle. Sometimes we stop by at Brumley's. If you'd like, we can convey your sympathies in that respect."

"Please do."

Dunbar and I walked to the livery stable and took out our horses. We led them for a walk and let them water at the trough at the town well. I let my gaze travel to the white house and earthen terrace of Richard Stanton and family. No one was in sight, but I felt as if Mrs. Stanton or one of the two perfect daughters could appear in an instant.

In spite of the gloomy interview with Mrs. Lancaster, Dunbar seemed to be in light spirits. He regarded the house with what I interpreted as a whimsical expression. He said, "I wonder how Hendy is getting along."

"It will be interesting to know."

We led the horses away from the water, tightened the cinches, and mounted up. As we rode north out of town, Dunbar spoke again.

"Rather serious lady, Mrs. Lancaster. Very civil, though."

I let my silence express my agreement.

"By now there are two women she doesn't resemble."

"Which ones are they?" I asked.

"The woman at the well, who had five husbands, and the woman taken in adultery."

"Which woman was that?"

"The one they wanted to stone, according to the old law. But Jesus said, 'He that is without sin among you, let him first cast a stone at her.' "

I thought I saw his point, not without a touch of humor, that Mrs. Lancaster was civil in forgiving someone for a sin she was not likely to commit herself. Then again, he might have been making an additional point about something that was beyond my understanding at that time.

CHAPTER EIGHT

We stopped at Brumley's on our way out to the range. The ranch yard was as desolate as ever, with the stillness broken only by the sound of a horse stamping to keep the flies off. Jack Brumley emerged from the shadowy interior of the barn, his eyes dark and heavy.

"Don't mean to bother you," said Dunbar, "but we thought we'd drop in to see if there's anything we can do to help out."

Jack raised his head to look up at us, squinting as sunlight fell on his haggard face. "Don't know what it would be. Thanks for askin', though."

Dunbar continued. "I'm sorry for what happened. I wish I could have done something at the time."

"Well, it's done, and no one can change it. And I don't know if anyone could have kept it from happening." I thought he meant that Kelso and Holcomb were determined to carry out their purpose. Then Jack added, "Some things seem as if they're written in the book."

I was struck by his sense of fatalism. I wondered if Dunbar believed in that sort of thing, but he did not respond to the idea.

Instead, he said, "We did speak with Jane Lancaster." He paused, as if waiting for a response, but none was visible. "She sends her sympathies."

Still with little expression, Jack said, "Thanks. She's all right, I guess."

After a few more seconds, Dunbar said, "Not much else at the moment. We're on our way to Carlyle's."

"Have a safe ride. Thanks for droppin' in."

When we had ridden over a hill and put the Brumley place behind us, I asked Dunbar, "Does it seem to you that Jack has some kind of a dislike for Mrs. Lancaster?"

"Could be. I've seen something of that nature before. A man's wife goes outside the bounds, and he resents her friends who might have known about it. Might not be fair on his part, but you can understand he would feel that way. Even if the friend didn't aid and abet, the friend knew things in confidence that the husband didn't. And in some cases, the friend might know personal details about the husband that are not all that flattering."

I felt an uneasiness at that idea. I said, "It's not a nice prospect to think about."

"No, it isn't. And unless a crime has been committed, it's best to close the door on that sort of thing."

Tom Carlyle was brushing the palomino horse in the shade of an elm tree when we rode into the yard. Motioning with the brush, he suppressed the uprising chickens and other fowl.

"Back from town," he said as we dismounted. "I heard the bad news about Willard Brumley. Makes me less and less comfortable about some of my neighbors."

Dunbar said, "It doesn't bode well at the present."

"Who's this new man Stanton has got there?"

"As far as I know, he's got two. One is a gunhand, and the other is a young fellow who looks like he might do ranch work."

"I don't know what to think about it. You know I've got my doubts about what happened to Ross, and now this shooting with Willard—"

"I think there might be some relation between the two, but I don't think it has anything to do with you, for what that might be worth."

Carlyle put his hand under Sunny's chin, as the horse had cozied up to him. "Of course I'm concerned about myself and whatever we've got here, but a man can't ignore what goes on around him. At least he shouldn't."

"I agree with you. And as long as we're here, I hope we can be of some use. We can take a ride out this afternoon and check on your cattle again. While we're at it, we'll keep an eye out for anything irregular."

"I appreciate it. Your place in the barn is the same as you left it."

"Thanks for letting me keep my second horse here."

"No trouble at all." Carlyle rubbed Sunny on the nose. "I'm going to finish with my own little pal, and I'll see about gettin' you fellas some grub before you go out."

Dunbar turned to me. "I think he's found out our secret. Always showing up at mealtime."

Carlyle spoke over his shoulder. "It's an old joke in the farm country where I came from. The boy tells on his father, says he whipped the horses to get there on time. But I don't see your horses sweatin' all that much."

"We know how to start out early. Don't want the horses to tell on us."

Dunbar and I rode out to the hardscrabble country where Carlyle's cattle grazed. We secured the same count as before, eleven cows and nine calves, and saw nothing out of order. In the hot, still afternoon, the country itself seemed changeless. At this time of year, one day was a replica of the day before. The various forms of life, from grass and sagebrush to dung beetles, grasshoppers, prairie dogs, jackrabbits, antelope, and cattle, all went about the business of keeping life going. I knew that life must feed on life, even in violent forms such as a coyote tearing apart a rabbit, but even with that knowledge, I felt that the natural rhythms of life in this broad grassland stood in contrast with the impulses of men, who stalked, baited, badgered, and killed their fellow men. Such men were aliens, I thought, and I hoped I would not become one of them.

Something hovered below the endless blue sky and above the rangeland that rolled away forever in all directions—something like a spell, especially on a summer afternoon when the only sounds were the dry footfalls of horses and the whirring of grasshoppers as they fled. My philosophical thoughts about man and nature subsided. The heavy air weighed on my eyelids, and half-remembered lines of poetry ran together in my head.

I widened my eyes. Dunbar had not spoken, but he had changed the course of the blue roan, and my horse had kept with them. Half a mile ahead, a windmill and a wooden tank sat in a depression with trampled ground on all sides.

I kept a rein on my horse as we rode forward. Ten yards from the tank, I dismounted and stretched, trying to shake off my drowsiness and pump up my circulation. The lazy afternoon held its own as the sun poured down its warmth. The blades of the windmill squeaked—or rather, the blades turned and the rod squeaked. I left my hat on my saddle horn and splashed my face in the warm tank water. When I was done, I stood back for Dunbar, who had taken off his hat and gloves. He bathed his face, then stood back and waved his hands to let them dry.

As on an earlier occasion, I saw the mark in the palm of his hand. I thought he noticed my seeing it, but as before, he made no attempt to conceal it. But he did speak in a way that diverted attention.

"The joke from farm country has gotten around. In the version I heard, the wife tells on him. I doubt that it makes a difference, and I wasn't going to mention it to Carlyle. His wife sends us out some pretty good grub."

"Yes, she does."

"Where do you think Hunton learned to cook? From his two wives, or in the Indian wars?"

I laughed. He caught me off guard. I said, "I don't know. I learned to eat what was put in front of me, but I have to admit it's not all the same."

"I trust Hunton not to poison us, though. Leave that to the folks who have way stations out where the law doesn't come by very often."

I found it encouraging to see Dunbar restored to his normal self. Here he was, under a calm, clear sky, far from the evils of his fellow man, recalling how people come to grief or bring misery upon one another.

When we returned to Carlyle's barn late that afternoon, we met a traveler who had arranged to put up for the night. He introduced himself as Bill Baker, and he said he was headed north to Montana. He was a slender man, below average height, with hazel eyes and a graying beard. He had a small saddle horse, a reddish bay about fourteen hands high, and a large white-and-tan donkey that was almost as tall as the horse. Bill was cheerful and friendly, and he did not ask us any questions about ourselves.

I noticed that he had a couple of instrument cases with the regular gear a traveler would carry on a pack animal. "Do you play music?" I asked.

"Yes, I do. I've got a banjo and a mandolin. And I can bang out a tune on a piano if there's one around. One thing about playin' music—unless it's caterwaulin' bad, people don't begrudge you a crust of bread or even a cup of refreshment. So if you fellows don't mind, I'll sing for my supper tonight. Like little Tommy Tucker, only it's old Bill Baker."

"Fine with me," I said.

"And me," said Dunbar.

The traveler took a seat where he could lean against his saddle and rummage around in his belongings. He brought out a pipe, a tobacco pouch, and a sardine can. He loaded his pipe with tobacco, lit it, shook out the match, and set the match with great care in the sardine can.

When he finished his pipe, he set it in the sardine can and took his mandolin from its case. After a few motions of picking and tuning, he launched into a simple melody and began singing a song called "The Little Mohee." It tells the story of a sailor who meets an Indian maiden, a chieftain's daughter. He turns down her offer of marriage and goes back to his home county, only to find that his original sweetheart has proven untrue. So he sails back over the ocean to his little Mohee.

I have heard this song many times since that first occasion, and whenever I hear it I recall the charm of the fanciful story and the pretty tune as the performance hung on the air in Tom Carlyle's barn and brought men of three different ages together.

After the song of the little Mohee, Bill sang "Bonny Barbara Allan," taking us through love and rejection, death and burial, and the growing together of the red rose and the briar. His version was a variation on others I had heard, but it was sad and sweet and wistful and all very nice. When Bill finished the song, applause came from the opening of the barn door.

"Well done, well done," said Tom Carlyle. "I wish there was room in the house, but we'll make do out here. Elsie has a pot roast, swimming with onions and potatoes. We'll be right out with it. She loves music as much as anyone does."

While Carlyle went back to the house, Bill worked his way into another song I had not heard before. He called it "Lorena," but it was not the song that begins, "The years slip slowly by, Lorena." It began:

Way down upon the old plantation
Old massa used to own me as a slave.
He had a yeller gal he called Lorena
And we courted where the wild bananas wave.

This song turned out also to be about separated lovers, as Lorena is sold away to old Virginny, and after many years, word comes back that she has died. The chorus is lovely and haunting, and I have learned it:

No more the moon shines on Lorena
As we'd sit and watch the coon among the corn
And the possum playing on the wild bananas
And the old owl a-hootin' like a horn.

As Bill sang the chorus the last time, Carlyle and his wife appeared with the pot, along with plates, knives, forks, and spoons.

"Hold it right there," said the host. "We'll be back with the bread and the pudding. Don't play another song yet, Bill. We don't want to miss any more."

The three of us sat in a pleasant atmosphere, with the aroma of the roast and the cooked vegetables wafting in the air. The Carlyles returned with a loaf of bread, a dish of butter, a cutting board, and an oven dish of baked pudding.

"Now we begin," said Carlyle. "Gentlemen, this is my wife, Elsie."

We all took off our hats. Mrs. Carlyle lowered her head in recognition, then stood up straight and smiled, as people do when they do not speak much of the local language.

By her demeanor, I thought her smile might be genuine. She had a beaming face, flushed at the moment from her exertion. She had reddish-yellow hair, wrapped in braids, and she had a sturdy yet feminine build. She looked quite capable of milking cows, herding geese, gathering eggs, and digging potatoes, but she also looked capable of collaborating with her husband to produce little Carlyles.

"Elsie hasn't been in this country very long," said our host. "So don't be surprised if you hear a few words in German."

The wife served our plates while the husband sliced bread. We all sat on wooden crates and enjoyed a sociable meal.

When everyone had finished with the main course, Carlyle said, "Now for the dessert. It's called Brown Betty." He held the dish in his lap as his wife spooned the pudding onto our plates. I could see, and then tell by tasting it, that it consisted of apples, bread, sugar, and spices such as nutmeg and cinnamon.

"It's kind of a bread pudding," said Bill.

"*Ya*," said Elsie. "Brett and apples."

The entire pudding disappeared in a few minutes. Tom and Elsie spoke to each other in a low tone, and the only word I picked up sounded like "beer." Elsie nodded, stood up, and walked to the house.

A few minutes later, she returned with a rectangular tray carrying a pitcher of beer and four glasses. Carlyle held the tray while his wife poured beer and handed out glasses.

"How about yourself?" said Bill.

Elsie smiled. "Later. This for you."

Bill held up his glass. "Well's here to a fine host and hostess."

A mutter of agreement went around.

Bill drank half of his glass and set it aside. "We'd better hear some more music," he said. He picked up his mandolin and warmed up again with a few notes.

The next number he sang was "Cowboy Jack," another sad song about lovers gone astray and separated by the death of the girl. Although I enjoyed these sentimental songs, I found them a bit indulgent, and I was beginning to wonder if they were Bill's favorite style. Then he surprised me, and perhaps the others, by saying he would like to play a song he wrote himself.

"That would be wonderful," said Carlyle. "We'd love to hear it."

Bill said, "So would I." He picked a couple of notes and said, "It goes like this."

On the rangeland the shadows grow longer
As the cattle bed down for the night,
And the call of the coyote at sunset
Comes alive with the dying of light.

In a cabin alone on the prairie
When another day's work is all done,
There's a soft, golden glow in the window,
And a maiden who sits all alone.

I imagine her dressed in warm flannel
As she combs her dark hair in the light,
And I poke at the coals in my campfire
As I sit 'neath the heavens so bright.

And I plan how I'll get things in order
When my work is all done in the fall,
And I'll head my good cow pony northward
As I'm drawn by that long silent call.

Then I'll hear the sharp cry of the coyote
As I hear it in this lonesome land,
As I think of the girl who is waiting
Way out on the Elsinore Grand.

In the meanwhile I'll put by some money
For a ring that I saw in Cheyenne—

Just a thin band of gold with a garnet
That will shine on my sweet darling's hand.

All my thoughts are of her in the distance,
As I work and save up as we planned
For the treasure of love that is waiting
Way out on the Elsinore Grand.

I was taken by this song, not only because I was young and idealistic but because it was plain and clear, with the notes ringing and the words falling together in a harmony that fit the rangeland itself.

When the last notes died away and the applause ended, Dunbar said, "That song has a pretty sentiment to it."

Bill said, "Thank you. It does, doesn't it?" With a nod in my direction he said, "A pretty song for young men's hopes." Then to Dunbar, "Meanin' yourself, as well."

"Of course. Drive dull cares away, as the earlier song said."

Bill drank from his glass of beer. "You bet. Drive away dullness, dread, and desperation. Of course, if you want any of that, there's songs to be heard." With that, he plucked a few notes from the mandolin and went into a song titled "Over the Hill to the Poorhouse." I had heard it before, but I had not noticed how dreadful and sentimental it was, as it went on about parents being left to die out in the cold or in the poorhouse as they are neglected by ungrateful children.

When Bill had finished the song and received his applause, Dunbar said, "In comparison with that song, 'Bury Me Not on the Lone Prairie' is an anthem of joy."

Bill perked up. "Oh, I can do that one, too." He picked, strummed, paused, and settled into the cadence of that mournful song. The dying youth with pale cold lips begs his comrades not to bury him in such a savage, lonely place, but they bury him there anyway, in a narrow grave just six by three, where the coyotes howl and the wind blows free. I imagined that each of us present lapsed into his or her own thoughts, for Elsie seemed delighted by the stately tune, while I could not keep myself from thinking about Willard.

Bill Baker was whistling "Sweet Betsy from Pike" as he loaded the packs on the white-and-tan donkey.

"What's this fella's name?" I asked as I rubbed the animal's nose.

"Ike. And my little pony here, his name's Aladdin."

"Are you sure you don't want some help?"

"No, thanks. I know where every little thing goes, and I've got all the details down to a routine. I'm used to doing it myself."

"We wish you safe travels," said Dunbar.

"Thanks. And the same to you fellas. Maybe we'll see you again, somewhere along the trail." Bill pulled on the lash rope, and the donkey grunted.

Dunbar's voice was cheerful. "We'll look for you out on the Elsinore Grand."

Bill smiled. "I might be there."

A few minutes later, Bill rode out of the yard, still whistling "Sweet Betsy from Pike." The cackling of Carlyle's chickens and the quacking of the ducks seemed as if they could have served as accompaniment for the song.

I turned to Dunbar and said, "What ideas do we have for today?"

"Small ones," he answered. "I need to ride that buckskin, so I thought I might go out and look at the country between here and the Clay Creek range."

"Out where we found Ross Guilford?"

"More or less. You're welcome to go along, of course, but you don't have to."

"I'll go. It'll do some good to ride my horse when there's nothing pressing. I get used to him, and he gets used to me."

"Not every horse is as easy to ride as that palomino, but you're doing all right with the little bay."

"Thanks," I said. "Heart of gold. By the way, Carlyle was right about Sunny. He does shift under you if you get off balance. Quite a difference from Blackie, who likes to turn sharp and send you sailing out across his shoulder."

"Is that what you've decided to name him, Blackie?"

"I think so."

We rode out east of Carlyle's place, where the grass appeared to be thicker when a rider looked across country at it than it did when he gazed straight down at it. As always, the terrain also had more variety than one would expect from the broad view. The land rose in gentle swells and gave way to new sights, sometimes grassy draws and sometimes rougher features.

After one such rise, we looked half a mile across country to a disruption in the earth. A jumble of rocks lay around an upthrust of low, mud-colored formations. As with other details, these columns were taller than I would have guessed at a distance until I saw that they rose well above the height of three men who were busy with something.

The tune of "Sweet Betsy from Pike" had been playing through my mind, with the comical references to the Shanghai rooster and the old yellow dog. Now the song vanished.

Dunbar and I rode toward the group of men. Halfway across the open ground, I counted horses and saw four. As the men moved around, I saw that there were four of them as well. I recognized Rich Stanton in his light-colored outfit, then two of the other men, Slater and Blythe. Closer, I identified the fourth man as the lanky young fellow who had stepped into the Dakota Rose.

I could not tell what the men were doing. They were making uncertain motions toward an area in the middle of the mud-like formations. At first I thought they might be throwing rocks at a rattlesnake, but then I saw that a couple of them had ropes and were making throws downward as if into a pit. Stanton stood back in an attitude of giving orders.

Dunbar and I kept our horses at a walk as we approached the site. One of the ranch horses whickered at ours, and Stanton turned to watch us as we rode the last few yards and came to a stop.

He said, "We've got a cow stuck down in a crevice."

"Do you need help?" asked Dunbar. "We'd be glad to lend a hand."

At that moment, the bellow of a cow rose up out of the cleft in the earth.

"Thanks all the same," said Stanton. "Any more would just crowd things. We're trying to get ropes on her and see if we can raise her up."

"Might be kind of hard. If she's in a crevice, you'll have to lift straight up. Even if she was in a bigger hole, you'd get a lot of resistance with her rubbing on the side of the hole."

"I know that."

"Do you mind if we take a look?"

"No, of course not. There's nothing other than what I said. A cow stuck down in some rocks."

Dunbar and I dismounted and held our horses by the reins as we walked up the slope, edged our way around the rocks, and peeked into the pit. In the dark interior I made out the shape of a brindle-colored cow with bony hips and a set of horns about a foot long on each side. Its eyes rolled, and its pink mouth opened, as it let out another bellow.

Slater said, "She's stuck good, and there's no gittin' down in there with her. It would be good to get a rope around her brisket, but I think the best we can do is loop one around each leg."

Blythe said, "Even if we get a couple of ropes on her, it's going to be hard to pull her out with horses because they can't pull straight up. It's going to be a hell of a drag."

The third cowhand, the gangling young man from the Dakota Rose, stood with his thumb hooked onto his belt as he held the rope at his side. He stared into the pit and said nothing.

Dunbar and I stepped out of the way as Slater threw a loop down into the hole and shook it.

Stanton spoke again. "A cow's worth money. I don't like to lose one this way. Bad enough to find one that died when you weren't around to do anything about it."

"Do you mind a suggestion?" said Dunbar.

"Not at all."

"I've heard of animals being trapped like this, and the men have gotten 'em out by raising the level of the floor."

Stanton frowned but kept his eyes on Slater as the hired man pulled up his rope and reshaped the loop. "What do you mean?" Stanton asked.

"By shoveling in dirt."

"My God," said Stanton, watching as Slater threw the rope downward again. "That would be a hell of a lot of dirt. And besides, we don't have any shovels with us, and this is all sandstone."

Dunbar said, "Silt stone. But no matter. It was just a thought."

"No harm done." Stanton still did not look at Dunbar as he spoke, and as on an earlier occasion, I had the impression that he would rather avoid a direct confrontation with Dunbar.

"You could even throw in some of these smaller pieces," Dunbar said.

Stanton did not say anything. He stared at the cow as Slater dangled his rope into the hole.

Dunbar broke the lull by saying, "Where's Kelso?"

Stanton flinched, then turned a calm face toward Dunbar and said, "He had to go to town. I think his mother's ailing back home, and he goes for the mail every couple of days."

"Oh," said Dunbar.

I thought a natural next question would entail whether Holcomb had to go with Kelso to check the mail, and I appreciated Dunbar's restraint in letting Stanton's bald statement hang in the air.

Slater said, "She stepped through the loop, so we've got a rope around one front leg."

"That's a start," said the boss. "We'll try to get two more, and then we'll see if we can raise her up."

"Gonna be hard even with three ropes."

"Of course it is. We've already said that enough times. If it was easy, we'd have had her out of there by now." Stanton turned his back on us, stepped to the edge of the hole, and peered down.

"I guess we'll go," said Dunbar.

Stanton did not answer.

Dunbar and I mounted up and paused. The gangling young man gave us a dull stare as the other three men looked down at the trapped cow.

"Good luck," said Dunbar, in a tone of farewell.

Blythe spoke over his shoulder. "Thanks."

Dunbar and I rode back toward Carlyle's. The tune of "Sweet Betsy from Pike" and the cartoon-like picture I had of a Shanghai rooster came back to my mind.

We rode without speaking until we had put a couple of swells of land between us and the Clay Creek men. Out of the blue, Dunbar said, "Some people don't like to take suggestions. They could ride back, fetch three shovels, carry the dirt a shovelful at a time, and still get that cow out sooner than trying to pull it up with ropes. But it's not our problem, I guess."

I was sure that Stanton's main reason for rejecting the advice was that it came from Dunbar. I thought Stanton's manner was curious, in that it seemed to me, at least, that Stanton avoided Dunbar yet all the time knew that his doing so was futile.

I looked at the sun. "It's early yet. What would you like to do next?"

"I know we just came from there, but I think we should go back to town. I didn't like the sound of what Stanton said about Kelso and his ailing mother."

CHAPTER NINE

Eva was cleaning up the last two tables after midday dinner. Her dark hair was plaited into a braid and hung between her shoulders in pretty contrast with her white blouse. She glanced around and smiled but kept at her work.

No customers sat at any of the tables, though some of the chairs had not yet been set straight into position. Muffled, unhurried sounds came from the kitchen, and in general, the Deville Café had a weary atmosphere of having been through a rush.

Medora came out into the dining area. She pulled in a breath as if she was summoning up a new supply of energy. Her eyes glanced downward, and she knelt to pick up a burned-out match.

"I wish they wouldn't do that," she said as she stood up. She moved over a couple of steps and set the matchstick on Eva's tray of used dishes. Turning back, she met us with a fresh smile. "And how are you two men today?"

Dunbar took off his hat with a sweep and said, "Happy are these eyes that see you, my lady."

She laughed. Eva and I met in a glance like two children whose parents were acting silly.

Medora said, "I haven't been to the theater in a few years. I miss it." Her dark eyes moved over us in a quick motion. "Please have a seat, won't you?"

Dunbar and I sat at a table next to the wall and set our hats aside. Medora struck a fetching pose in her white blouse and black skirt, with a hand on her hip and with her chin raised.

"So, is this a time for pie and coffee, or would you like a full meal?"

Dunbar gazed up at her. "I believe I could get by on pie and coffee. But we'll see what my *segundo* says."

As I was the only person he could be referring to, I said, "That's fine with me."

"We're limited to rhubarb today," she said. "I hope that's all right."

We both assured her it was, so she went back to the kitchen.

As we sat without speaking, I realized I had a different tune running through my head. "Sweet Betsy from Pike" had given way to "Lorena," the melancholy song about the slave whose master sells Lorena and she is taken away to old Virginny.

"Something wrong?" said Dunbar.

He must have read my face. "Oh, no," I said. "I was just remembering one of those sad songs we heard from Bill Baker."

"He's a good one, isn't he?"

"Yes, he is. He must know a thousand songs."

A bell sounded, and the front door opened. We both turned to see Pat Hendy strolling in. He did not have the air of a man in search of dinner, and I knew he stayed at the Waverly Hotel and took his meals there. He pulled out a chair at the table before ours and was about to sit down when Dunbar hailed him.

"Why don't you sit with us, Pat?"

"Oh, I guess I could." He dragged the chair around and set it at the end of our table, as we had the other two chairs hemmed in.

Dunbar maintained a cheery tone as he said, "We just came in off the range. What's new in the world?"

Hendy shifted in his chair, then looked up over his shoulder as Medora appeared with two cups of coffee. He said, "I guess I can tell everyone at once. I'm leaving town."

"That's too bad," said Dunbar. "Did the job fall through?"

"It did just that. I thought Mrs. Stanton wanted the work done, but in the end I think it was her husband who put the kibosh on it."

"Money?" asked Dunbar.

"That's usually it."

Medora spoke. "Coffee, Pat?"

"I believe I will. Thanks."

"These two gentlemen are having pie. Would you like some?"

"No, thanks. Just coffee."

When Medora left, Dunbar said, "I'm sorry to hear you didn't get the work."

"I put quite a bit of effort into the plans, the cost estimate, and all, and then to be turned away—but, that's business." He took me in with a perfunctory smile. "Made some friends here, too."

"Maybe we'll meet again," said Dunbar.

"You never know." He smiled at Medora as she set a cup of coffee in front of him. Then he spoke to Dunbar. "Maybe I'll come back, or maybe we'll meet somewhere else. It's a small world at times."

"Isn't it, though?" said Dunbar.

"Small, but not always easy to figure out." Hendy's spirits seemed to be picking up. He smiled again at Medora as she appeared and stood back with our two orders of pie. He looked at Dunbar and said, "You told me before that you're a cowpuncher. Have you done that all your life?"

"Not yet."

Medora laughed, and I did, too.

Hendy said, "That's good."

I thought he meant the joke was good, but I wasn't sure. Medora set down our two small plates, and I turned my attention to my pie. From the corner of my vision I saw Medora leave us to our company.

Dunbar spoke. "You say you might come back. Did you hear anything from Mr. Rutledge about the township he's planning?"

"Madeleine? Oh, yes. He mentioned it. He said he offered you a chance to work there, and of course I put in a word for myself." He took a sip of coffee. "If they would get a surveyor in there, why, with some men and the right equipment, I could scrape out some streets in a matter of a few days." He punched Dunbar on the shoulder. "You bet. You'd be a good man on the job. We could move some dirt together."

Dunbar said, "You never know." After a second, he continued. "As you said last time, every good man has it in him to be more than one thing. I could set aside the cowhand trade and hold the measuring stick while you peeped through the transit."

Hendy's full face lit up as he laughed. "That would be just it." He settled down from his laughing. "We could do it, though. It's one thing I know about."

"I know you do. By the way, being, as you are, a man who moves dirt, I wonder if you've heard the story of the donkey in the well."

"Not that I recall."

"I believe it's a true story. I've told it before, but not to you, so here it is. There was a farmer who had an old donkey, and one day the animal fell down in an abandoned well. The farmer had no idea of how to get him out, and since the animal was old and not very useful, and the well was no longer in use, the farmer decided he would bury the donkey there. So he started to pour in dirt, but every time he dumped in a wheelbarrow load, the animal shook himself off and climbed up onto the new floor of dirt. Little by little, the farmer raised the level of dirt until the donkey climbed out on his own."

I thought Dunbar might be a little stubborn in not letting go of his suggestion of how to get the cow out of the hole, but he knew his audience.

Hendy smiled and said, "That's a good story to remember. Usually you take the dirt out of the hole." He tipped his head in consideration. "You know, donkeys are good beasts of burden. They've hauled a lot of ore out of mines, especially down in Mexico."

"They sure have. Your mention of Mexico reminds me of another story about a donkey. This is not what they call a true story. I heard it in Spanish, but it translates pretty well."

"Sure. Let's hear it." Hendy looked at me and made a close-mouthed smile that lifted his bristly mustache.

Dunbar began. "A fellow goes to his friend's house and sees a crowd of people there. He says to his friend, 'What are all these people doing here? Did someone die?' His friend says, 'Yes, my mother-in-law died.' The fellow says, 'Oh, that's too bad. What did she die of?' The friend says, 'She got kicked in the head by a burro.' 'Oh, that's terrible. And this is a lot of people. Did your mother-in-law have that many friends?' 'Oh, no,' says the friend, 'they all came to see about buying the burro.' "

Hendy started jiggling with laughter. He said, "Oh, that's too good. Sometimes people from other countries have different kinds of jokes than we do." He laughed some more and settled down. "Sometimes the stories seem heartless, but like you say, they translate all right. I don't speak French, but I heard one that started out in that language, or at least that's what I was told. It's about two cannibals, eating from a big pot of soup. The first one says, 'I *hate* my mother-in-law.' The second one says, 'That doesn't matter. Just eat your carrots.' "

"That's good, too," said Dunbar.

"They both are. But if we get the job of movin' dirt in the

town of Madeleine, we won't tell these jokes to Mr. Stanton. Or to Mr. Rutledge, either. Actually, I think he might take it to heart more than his son-in-law would." Hendy looked around. "Not to be crying over spilt milk, but I think he's a bit cold. The son-in-law, that is." He reached into his vest pocket. "By the way, here's my card."

Dunbar took it. "Thanks."

Medora returned with a coffeepot and filled our cups. She said, "Sorry to hear you're leaving, Pat."

"So am I."

From the glimmer in his eyes I interpreted a purpose for his visit. He had come to say goodbye to Medora.

She said, "That's the way life goes. If you come back to town, drop in, of course."

"I'll be sure to."

Out on the street in the afternoon sunlight, Dunbar said, "We haven't found out very much so far, just that Stanton doesn't want Hendy to move dirt, and Rutledge might."

"Was there something you were expecting?"

"Not in particular. It was just a feeling I had." He had put on his gloves, and now he smoothed his mustache. "I think I'd like to check on Mrs. Lancaster and see how she is doing."

"Do you think she has more to say?"

"I think she knew more than she told us, but that doesn't mean she has anything she cares to share with us. But it's worth a visit." Dunbar glanced at the sun, then up and down the street. "Let's go on foot again."

We left the horses tied in front of the café and walked the short distance to Jane Lancaster's house. The shades were drawn as before, and the house was drab and inexpressive.

After knocking on the door twice and receiving no answer, Dunbar gave me a questioning look and tried the door handle.

The door opened inward, and I caught a whiff of stale but cooler air.

"I guess we'll go in," said Dunbar.

The dim interior was matched by the total silence of the house. We passed through the living room, which had the spare furnishings I had seen on our earlier visit. An open doorway led into the kitchen, where the light was a little brighter. I followed Dunbar until he stopped short inside the kitchen. I moved to his side and stared at the floor, where the body of Jane Lancaster lay still. The woman lay on her side with one leg bent at the knee and one arm stretched outward with the palm up.

A light dizziness, a detached sense of reality, took hold of me. From the first second, I had no doubt that she was dead. What impressed me was the certainty, the absolute immobility of the body. She lay as if she had fallen or had been dropped there. As I stared, I became aware of what was not present—no blood, no wounds, no kitchen items or furniture in disorder.

Dunbar knelt by the body, took off his right glove, and made minimal contact on the victim's neck and chin. He stood up and pulled his glove back onto his hand.

"She's cold and rigid. She's been dead a while, at least several hours. It looks like strangulation, but I'm not a coroner."

My senses were still swimming. I could comprehend the physical details, but the reason for the death made no sense at all. I said, "I don't understand why someone would do this to an old lady who didn't bother anyone."

"As you know, I don't like to speak ahead of time. But I think we can say this isn't something all by itself."

I stared at the body, trying to make sense of it. "What shall we do?"

"Report it," said Dunbar.

I frowned. "We don't have any police. I can't even remember a deputy sheriff coming through."

"From what I gather, Mr. Rutledge is the closest thing to a mayor in this town, so I'll report it to him. He can send for or bring in a deputy."

"What shall I do?"

"You don't need to go with me if you don't want."

My eyes opened wide at the stark scene in the kitchen. "Do you want me to stay here?"

Dunbar frowned as he glanced around at the floor. "I don't think you'd enjoy it here, and I don't think it's good for one person to be in a situation like this without another person present. As a witness. We don't want someone to come back and say you changed something."

I felt a small wave of relief. "Shall I stay with the horses, then?"

He looked up. "That's as good a place as any. I shouldn't be gone for long."

We left the dusky scene of death and stepped out into the sunlight. I was still in a daze as we walked to the horses and Dunbar took off on his own, leaving me alone in the street. A block away, a woman lay dead inside the small, dim world of her house, while out under the open sky, life went on all around me. Life and more death. This was the third death I had seen in a week, and no two of them were alike. Meanwhile, as I stood in the street, birds chirped, horses stamped at flies, smoke rose from stovepipes, and a hammer somewhere in town went *rap-rap-rap*.

A bell sounded as the front door of the café opened behind me. I turned around to see Eva, dressed in her white blouse and black skirt. Her dark hair was twined in a braid as it had been earlier, and it swayed beyond her shoulder as she walked. She stepped off the sidewalk and stood near enough to speak in a low voice.

"Has something happened?" Her eyes showed concern.

"What have you heard?"

"Only that something happened."

I frowned as my eyes moved away from her. "I haven't seen anyone on the street spreading news."

"It came down the back alley."

My eyes came back to hers, then took in the whiteness of her blouse, the darkness of her hair. I wanted to be close to her, to be the person who knew things she wanted to know. Dunbar had not told me to keep a tight lip, but my own sense of caution kept me in check.

I said, "I need to wait until Dunbar comes back."

"You look worried."

"I don't know what to think."

She patted the buckskin on the neck. "Is this Mr. Dunbar's horse?"

"Yes, he has two."

"I've seen the other one. And this dark horse that you ride."

I took it as a good sign that she noticed horses and kept track of them. I was trying to think of what to say when a sharp voice chilled me.

"You'd better move along, little girl."

Holcomb had appeared out of nowhere, and here he stood a yard away in the street. I thought he must have come from the center of town, but I wondered if he had stepped out from the shade of a building, in which case he would have heard what we said.

Eva and I both stared at him.

"Move along," he said, with a motion of his head. "Make yourself scarce."

My heartbeat moved into my throat, and my mouth was dry. I nodded to Eva, and she turned to go back into the café. I lost sight of her as she slipped into the shadows.

Holcomb trained his eyes on me. His hat shaded his upper

face, but his blue-gray eyes with their puffy lower eyelids bored into me. His forward-leaning posture and his hook nose brought his nickname to my mind. Holcomb the Hawk.

"What do you think you're doing, you little snot?"

My heart was beating fast, and I tried to keep my voice calm. "Waiting here."

He stepped forward, his hawkish beak not two feet away from me. "Waitin' for what? A passenger train?"

"I don't know."

"You don't know. I guess you don't. Taggin' along with a smugger that's goin' to get you hurt. You don't know him or what he's up to." Holcomb's voice took on a malicious edge. "Do you?"

I felt as if I had been stuck with a knife. "No."

"You don't know a damn thing. But people get hurt for it anyway. If you knew what was good for you, you'd get the hell out of here and stay gone." His voice turned sharp again. "Don't you think?"

My mouth had gone even drier, and my heart was pounding. My voice was shaky as I said, "I don't know."

He reached over with his left hand, grabbed my upper arm with his thumb and forefinger, and gave a twist to my skin.

I jerked away and said, "Ouch!"

"Ha, ha. You'd make a good cabin boy."

I knew what a cabin boy was from having read *Treasure Island,* but I did not think that was his meaning. Later in life I would come to understand the coarser use of the expression and would remember Holcomb in the sunny, dusty street of Dry Camp. For the moment, I said nothing.

The Hawk kept it up. "I see you're wearin' a gun."

I swallowed hard and said, "I have a right to."

"Of course you do. Just like women have a right to wear

men's clothes." His voice cut into me again. "Do you know how to use it?"

"Not much." I tried to keep my answer short so he wouldn't hear the quaver in my voice.

"Then you shouldn't wear it. Maybe you should take it off." When I didn't answer, his menacing tone came back. "Talk to me."

"I don't have anything to say."

"You wear a gun, and you don't know how to use it. Maybe I should show you."

My heartbeat felt as if it was in my ears. I remembered Willard and how Holcomb would not let up on him. I felt paralyzed, not knowing what to do or say.

"I don't like it when someone doesn't answer me."

"You didn't ask a question."

"Maybe I will, then. I said, maybe I should show you how to use your gun. What do you think of that?"

I summoned up an answer. "I don't think it's necessary."

"But you don't know much. What you think might not be very accurate. So we'll do it this way. I'll just tell you what to do rather than ask you questions. Do you understand me?"

"Yes, I do." I could feel my hand shaking, and I did not hold it anywhere near my pistol handle.

"Then we'll do it like this. I want you to take out your six-gun and show it to me."

I was petrified. I could not move. I thought that if I took out my gun, I would drop it. And if I didn't drop it, he would see me shaking so bad he would laugh. As I had these thoughts, something deeper told me not to touch my gun. This was the man who shot Willard Brumley.

My head was swimming worse than before. I could not do anything. I hoped Eva was inside the café and could not hear any of what was going on.

Holcomb's tense voice came back. "I told you to take out your six-gun and show it to me." His hawk eyes bored into me as he waited.

Time seemed to draw out at a tenth of its regular speed. I could not move my hand even if I wanted to. Then time changed as Holcomb grabbed me by the front of my shirt and pulled me down to the tip of his nose.

"Now you look here, you little guttersnipe."

His voice was cut off by a louder, outside voice. "Let him go," said Dunbar.

Holcomb's hand relaxed on my shirt, and I settled back onto my feet. Holcomb turned and squared away, as if he was going to shoot it out right there with Dunbar.

Holcomb said, "You can keep out of this, partner."

"I'm no partner of yours, and I won't keep out of things when someone like you is pickin' on a boy like this."

A sneer crept onto Holcomb's face. "Someone like me. Now what might you mean by that?"

"I think you might know. You know what you've done."

"Maybe I don't. What have you heard?"

"I don't need to go any farther than what I've seen. You pushed Willard Brumley into a fight, and then you shot him down."

Holcomb's voice was as tight as high-strung barbed wire. "Mister, I don't let nobody pull a gun on me."

I was surprised to hear Holcomb being so sure of himself, more so than either Stanton or Kelso, and I imagined it was because Dunbar had not interfered much when Holcomb was harassing Willard.

Dunbar gave Holcomb a cold look of appraisal. He said, "And I don't let anyone push around a kid just because he rides with me."

Holcomb swayed his body side to side as he stepped closer to

Dunbar. "Maybe that's not the only—"

"Don't crowd me."

Holcomb stopped and laughed. "I'll do as I please."

"Don't be too sure." The finality in Dunbar's voice seemed to stop time for a second.

"Huh." Holcomb stepped back half a pace. "One of these days, you'll push things too far."

Dunbar spoke in a steady voice. "Don't be so sure of thinking you know how things will turn out."

"I just know your type. I don't predict the future."

"You're better off that way."

Holcomb raised his head and lowered it. "One of these days you might get the surprise of your life." He pivoted on his heel and walked away.

Dunbar and I stood in silence until Holcomb had reached the corner and crossed to the next block. The man had taken warning and had rephrased his threat, but I did not see him as leaving in retreat. I thought he was still sure he could take Dunbar at a moment of his choosing.

Dunbar said, "I came in at the end of your . . . encounter."

"He tried to get me to take out my gun and show it to him."

"It's a good thing you didn't."

A chill ran across my shoulders as I recalled that moment when I knew not to touch my gun. I said, "Do you think he would have used it as an excuse to—?" I could not bring myself to finish the question.

Dunbar said, "I don't know. But we saw what he did with Willard. Whatever he was up to with you, you can be sure it was no good."

I wanted to ask why, but I was afraid that the answer, even if it was "I don't know," would put me in the same group as Ross Guilford, Willard Brumley, and Jane Lancaster.

CHAPTER TEN

The Reverend Mansfield conducted a brief service for Jane Lancaster at the town cemetery. The Reverend spoke in a calm, even tone, discoursing on the briefness of our lives and the uncertainty of our end. Because no one knew the manner of his going, each of us should be prepared ahead of time, believing in the Lord and accepting him as the only salvation. For without Him we are lost, adrift on an endless sea in a shroud of fog.

The Reverend delivered his message on a sunny, breezy afternoon at the edge of town, his back to a sea of grass. Jane Lancaster's wooden coffin sat next to a plain dirt grave, and I fancied that the coffin was like a ship about to embark on a journey—not to be locked in ice like the ships of the lost Franklin Expedition, but to be stuck in a hummock and drifted over with dirt.

My eyes came back to the grave itself, and my fancy was replaced by a more realistic idea. Jane Lancaster was being buried on the lone prairie, in a narrow grave just six by three, where the coyotes howl and the wind blows free.

I had not been to many funerals at that point in my life, but I was used to the preacher taking advantage of the occasion and delivering a sermon on the necessity of belief, repentance, and acceptance. I was surprised, however, when he ended on a more personal note.

"We do not know the state of Jane's soul. She was not known to be a believer, but it is difficult for me to imagine anyone but a depraved miscreant not to be aware of God's workings. For her sake, I hope she had some such awareness. God leaves his print on every human heart, and few there be who do not feel it."

The Reverend drew a breath and paused, looking over our small group. He was a pale-complexioned man in a dark hat and suit, silhouetted against a large and empty land, but he was not timid. He continued. "As for her dying by hands unknown, that was the work of a coward, not a punishment for her time on earth. God does not punish in that way. For Jane's sake, I hope that the person or persons who took her life will be brought to justice. Be that as it may, they will certainly face the highest justice of all. And on that note of hope, our service is ended."

I felt a release, a burden lifted, and I felt in unison with the other people gathered on that little knoll. Then the elation subsided and we became a group of individuals shaking hands with the preacher, nodding to one another, putting on our hats, and dispersing. As was sometimes my habit when I did not know what else to do, I counted. In addition to Dunbar, Ambrose Lennox, and myself, Jane Lancaster's mourners consisted of Medora, two women from town whose names I did not know, Hunton the innkeeper, and Jack Brumley, who had arrived at the end. Eight, plus the preacher.

Dunbar and I stayed with Lennox as the rest trailed away. The old man looked worse than ever with his thinning white hair and pale scalp, purple nose, and yellow eyes. His shoulders slumped, and his belly sagged. He picked at a flake of dead skin on his right cheekbone and stared at the ground.

"I thought the preacher made something good out of it," Dunbar offered.

Lennox sniffed. "I suppose so. But I didn't think he had to make so much out of her being a nonbeliever. What she did with her own life was her business."

His words summoned in my mind an image of Jane Lancaster in life, not as I had seen her on the kitchen floor—plain and not very feminine, with short gray hair, not well trimmed, and a drab complexion save for her small, red nose. I did not have an idea of what her life might have or have not included. I did know she helped women and had a level of confidence with them, and as such, she may not always have been appreciated by men. It occurred to me, then, that what Lennox was defending in her was a characteristic they shared. They were not misfits, for a small country town could accommodate more people at its edges than a city person might expect, but they lived their lives in ways that kept them out of the center of what could be called society. No one was going to name a town after either of them.

Dunbar must have been thinking along some of the same lines. He said, "I'm sure she did a great deal of good for many women."

Lennox raised his hand with a slight wave. "You're damn right she did."

"And I would imagine she heard things in confidence."

"Oh, I'm sure of that."

"When I spoke with her that last time, you know, we talked about Louise Brumley."

"She knew Louise."

"Of course. You told us that before. That's why we went to see her."

I wondered at Dunbar treating Lennox like a forgetful old drunk, and yet I could appreciate his always keeping the record straight.

Lennox had assumed his morose expression again. He rubbed his nose and said, "I know."

Dunbar kept the conversation in stride. "She told us a little about Louise. Not everything she knew, I don't think, but a little. Among the things she told us was that someone here in town reported seeing Louise in North Platte, in the company of some man who had been seen around town here."

"Oh, yes, I remember that. They figured he hung around here because he was seeing her. And then she took off with him."

"No idea of the man's name, though?"

"Not that I recall. If someone had known it, it would have kicked around and been remembered."

"That's what I would think."

Silence hung in the little cemetery. The breeze riffled through Lennox's thinning hair. The shadow of a cloud darkened a spot on the grassland to the north.

Dunbar spoke again. "Do you remember who reported seeing them there?"

"In North Platte?" Lennox pushed his lips outward. "It was a long time ago, but I believe it was Rich Stanton. He had gone there to buy something for his wedding. I don't remember what."

"Did they have the wedding here?"

"Oh, no. They all went back to Des Moines. That's where Rutledge is from, you know."

"Is that where Madeleine is buried? I don't see her here." Dunbar motioned with his head toward the other graves.

Lennox's eyes opened. "Oh, yeah. She even died there. Where they have the best doctors." His eyes fell. "For us common folks, this place is good enough, I guess. When you're dead, you're dead. I think that's how Jane saw it."

Dunbar glanced at the open grave. "Someone will come to do the actual burial, then?"

"Uh-huh. The barber takes care of that. He came out earlier and dug the grave. He'll come back when everyone's gone."

Lennox took a deep breath with his mouth open. "I suppose we've done as much good as we're going to. What do you say we go have a drink to the memory of my friend Jane?"

"I suppose we can do that," said Dunbar.

I nodded. I had a lump in my throat, and I didn't have much to say anyway.

Lennox regarded the coffin with a direct stare, made something like a salute, and said, "So long, Jane." He rubbed his eyes with both hands and then joined us for the walk back to town.

The Dakota Rose had three patrons standing at the bar, rough-looking fellows who wore the clothes of teamsters or ditch grad-ers. Men of that cut would pass through from time to time, so I did not pay them much attention as Dunbar, Lennox, and I sat at our usual table.

Lennox let out a long, weary breath. "I'm gettin' too old for some of this," he said.

Dunbar sounded a dubious note as he said, "Going into saloons?"

"No. Going to funerals. It just occurred to me that it's been twenty-five years since my brother Calvin died."

"Sorry to hear that," said Dunbar.

"No way to change it. Healthy young fellow, then he up and got tuberculosis."

"That's a terrible one. It gets a lot of 'em."

"It sure does."

The bartender appeared with a glass of whiskey and two glasses of beer. "How's this?" he asked.

"Just right," said Dunbar.

As the bartender faded away, Lennox took a sip and said, "Ahhh." He blinked his eyes. "I guess I got ahead of us." He raised his glass and said, "Here's to my old friend, Jane."

Dunbar and I raised our glasses to meet in the toast, then settled back into our chairs. A few minutes passed, and the atmosphere relaxed. Lennox finished his whiskey in four or five swallows, spread not far apart. His hand was steady, and his voice had smoothed out. I have met men like him since then. With some trace of the elixir always in their veins, it doesn't take much to bring them back up to a level of round edges and smooth flowing.

"Can't stay glum forever," he said. He signaled for another drink. "Calvin wouldn't want me to, and neither would Jane. Life is for the ones who are still living. I said the same thing to Pat Hendy when he was talking about Rutledge's dead wife. Now he was a good one, Hendy. I wonder where he is now."

Dunbar said, "I would imagine he's at his next job."

"Ha-ha. He might be sittin' in a saloon at this very minute, tellin' stories."

"He might be."

"Here's one he told me, after I said life was for the living. He said he met a girl who was all sad because her sweetheart died. Didn't know if she could ever love again. He asked her what the fella died of, and she said he fell off a scaffold. So Hendy was interested. He asked what the fella was doin' on the scaffold when he fell off, and the girl said, 'Gettin' hanged.' "

Lennox began laughing. I could see the humor, but it did not move me or Dunbar that far. I supposed Lennox needed something to laugh at, and his priming of whiskey helped.

I was hoping that Dunbar would come up with a story or a comment, but the scene changed as two men passed through the light of the open doorway. My pulse jumped as I recognized Kelso and Holcomb.

The bartender set down Lennox's drink and returned to his place behind the bar. I stole a glance as he poured whiskey for the two new customers.

I looked at Dunbar, who was alert, and at Lennox, who had a dull, contemptuous expression on his face.

"There's no good in this," said Lennox.

Dunbar spoke in a low voice. "Leave it alone. Don't pay any mind."

"They'd better leave us alone."

"They've got no reason not to."

I felt Dunbar made his statement out of a sense of obligation to keep things calm at our table. A minute later, I had cause to believe I was right.

Kelso and Holcomb left their drinks on the bar and came swaggering our way. Kelso's spurs jingled, but as I had noticed before, Holcomb did not wear spurs. His approach was quieter.

They stopped at about a yard from our table. Kelso had his thumbs on his belt, and he held his head back. With his upper lip tight, he said, "Afternoon, men. I hope you're all well."

Dunbar and I nodded as Lennox sulked.

Kelso continued. "I thought I would return the favor. Boss said you asked about me the other day."

"Just bein' polite," said Dunbar.

"That's the best way. So how's everything out at Carlyle's?"

"All right, the last time we checked."

"Sure. Even a small herd of cattle needs to be checked on. Good thing is, it gives you time to come to town and sit around in barrooms."

Dunbar set his beer glass a few inches farther away. "Some jobs are like that."

"Seems as if it gives you time to keep track of other people as well." Kelso had his arms at his sides now as his chest went up and down once. "Boss said you were askin' about my whereabouts."

"Just a friendly question. I thought that if you were there, they might have gotten that cow out of the hole a little quicker."

"Thoughtful of you."

"The way I learned my trade. Every cow is important."

Holcomb had edged forward and leaned now like a hawk on a fencepost. With his eyes fixed on Dunbar, he said, "Your trade. Just exactly what is your trade, mister?"

"I'm a cowpuncher."

"Well, I haven't seen you do much of it."

Dunbar's eyes were calm as he gave Holcomb a look of appraisal. "I don't know how much you've followed me around."

"You're startin' to get cheeky with me again."

Lennox had been following the conversation back and forth like an old dog with sad eyes. At this point he blurted, "Talk about cheeky."

Holcomb shifted and leaned toward the old man. "What business is it of yours?" he asked.

Spit flew from Lennox's lips. "Pick, pick, pick. You make me sick the way you pick away at a man. Just tryin' to push him into a fight."

"Stand up."

A wave of dread flowed through my body. I could see Dunbar turning.

Lennox said, "Ah, you're a brazen son of a bitch."

Holcomb's tongue appeared between his lips, then disappeared. "Stand up," he said. "I'm givin' you a chance to take that back."

Lennox still had his hand on his drink as he rose from his chair. In a jerky motion, he flung the whiskey in Holcomb's face.

Chairs scraped and bumped as Dunbar and I scrambled to our feet. At the same time, Holcomb snatched Lennox by the front of his shirt, flung him to the floor, and held him down with a boot on the chest.

"Leave the old man alone," said Dunbar.

"I'm not done with him. You heard what he called me, and you saw what he did."

Lennox's voice rose on the air. "I just wish it was a cup of piss."

Holcomb pushed down with his boot. "You miserable old son of a bitch. I should twist your neck like an old rooster."

"Pffft. You must think I know too much. Like the others."

Holcomb moved his foot so that his boot pushed down on Lennox's neck. The old man's eyes opened wide.

Dunbar stood up. "Leave him alone," he said. "He's no match for you."

"You stay out of it. If he can't take care of himself, he should learn to keep his mouth shut." Holcomb raised his hand to wipe the whiskey from his face. When he finished, he narrowed his eyes and pressed down harder with his foot.

At the edge of my vision, I saw the three rough-looking men at the bar, all watching.

Lennox began to make rasping, choking sounds.

Dunbar moved to intervene. "That's enough." He put his shoulder against Holcomb and pushed him off balance.

Holcomb turned to make a grab at Dunbar's arm, as much to regain his balance as to fight back. Meanwhile, Kelso stepped across Lennox to rush Dunbar from the other side.

For once I acted without hesitating. I lunged forward and blocked Kelso from laying hold of Dunbar. I knocked Kelso off balance, and I think it took him by complete surprise, for he pulled his gun as he regained his footing, and only then did he seem to recognize me.

Things froze between Kelso and me. Within a few seconds, Dunbar and Holcomb had drawn apart and moved back from the line of fire. When everything first froze, I felt as if my heart had stopped, but now it was pounding.

"What's the gun for?" said Dunbar.

Kelso's upper lip was tight as the corners of his mouth pulled down. "Someone hit me on my blind side."

"You want to be careful pullin' a gun. It gives someone else a right to do the same."

Kelso's nostrils flared. "Let him try. He's packin' one."

"How much of a chance do you think there is of that?"

Kelso did not answer. His glance flickered toward the bar where the three other men stood. As the seconds ticked by, his standing there with a gun drawn seemed more and more like a pointless gesture.

The whole commotion had taken place in about a minute. The bartender was the same man who had been on duty when Willard was shot, and he must have been keeping his distance. With the action now at a lull, he called out across the space of fifteen feet.

"Mind out, now. We're not going to have any more trouble."

Holcomb moved back half a step and stood up straight. "No trouble at all."

Kelso put his gun in his holster and rested his hand on the butt. "Nope," he said. "None at all. Just returnin' a courtesy."

The two of them strode back to the bar as Lennox rose from the floor. He had his elbow raised as he rubbed the side of his neck. He frowned at the empty glass on the table.

The three of us sat down. In a soft tone, Dunbar said, "We don't need any more of that."

"I know," said Lennox. "But the sons of bitches make me mad." He moved his mouth back and forth. "I need a drink." After signaling to the bartender, he spoke to us in a low voice. "I meant it when I said he was brazen. I don't think I'm the only one in this town that thinks they had somethin' to do with what happened to Jane."

Dunbar said, "That may be, but there's better ways of going about it."

★ ★ ★ ★ ★

The lobby of the Waverly Hotel had a cool and placid atmosphere. The rug on the hardwood floor muffled our steps, and the voices from the kitchen area were subdued. Silver-haired Gilbert Rutledge stood behind the oak reception desk, neat and trim in a light blue suit. He held a brass letter knife in one hand and rested the tip on the other hand, poised as if we had brought a letter for him to open.

"A pleasure again to see you," he said as we came to a stop.

"And a pleasure on our part as well," said Dunbar.

"Something I can help you with? A room?"

I assumed he knew we put up in the more modest lodgings of Mr. Hunton, and I imagined he was making an oblique comment about it. At the same time, I thought he might have been pretending not to be aware of our more probable purpose.

Dunbar said, "Thank you, but we're here on the same cause as the last time I came by."

Rutledge's blue eyes moved from Dunbar to me and back to Dunbar. "Oh, yes. The death of that woman. Terrible thing."

"I was wondering if anyone has made progress on the case."

Rutledge lifted his eyebrows. "In what way?"

"As I mentioned before, you are the closest thing this town has for a mayor, and I was hoping you might send for someone in the sheriff's office. Just trying to prompt things, you understand. Not presuming to tell anyone what to do."

"Of course. And any citizen has a right to be concerned."

"Yes, and it's been three days. We wouldn't want to see things languish."

"That long already." Rutledge exhaled a small breath. "There's always so much to do that it's hard to find time. I haven't forgotten about it, and to tell you the truth, I've been thinking of doing it. But it's not the only thing I have to do. And I don't know if you're aware of this, but it's a good fifteen-

155

mile trip each way to send a telegraph. It's not like walking across the street."

"Have you thought of sending someone?"

"I suppose I could, but everyone I know is busy."

I pictured Kelso and Holcomb, who seemed to have enough time to hang around town. I hoped Rutledge would not suggest them, though I doubted he would, given what he had said about Kelso in our first meeting.

"I'll go," said Dunbar.

"How's that?"

"I said I'll go. You can write the message, put it in a sealed envelope, and I'll deliver it by myself. Clean as that. No conspiracy."

Rutledge gave a small laugh. "I wouldn't expect any."

I thought he was glad to have gotten through the topic, but Dunbar had a little more to say.

"I realize that Mrs. Lancaster was not a prominent citizen, but any suspicious death like this one matters."

"Oh, of course. If we can't tend to this, who are we, uh?"

Prior to leaving town, Dunbar took the initiative of asking Medora if I could spend a few hours at the café, out of the way. I felt like a child whose parent was putting him under someone else's care for the day, but when Medora said I could help Eva peel potatoes, I accepted my lot. And so I found myself sitting on the back steps in the shade, in the pleasant company of Eva Beaulieu and a large pan of potatoes.

"I'm sorry if Mr. Dunbar stuck you with women's work," she said.

"Oh, no," I answered, though I felt clumsy with my six-gun clunking against the wooden step where I sat. "As for peeling potatoes or scrubbing pots and pans, those are the kinds of things a wrangler does."

"A wrangler?"

"Yes. That's the level where a young fellow starts out at ranch work. He takes care of the horses, and he helps the cook. Out on roundup, I gather firewood, fetch water, and do whatever else the cook tells me."

"Then you're not too proud to do low work."

"I don't know if it's low, but it's lower-level."

"That's what I meant."

"Sure. And, no, I'm not too proud. I started out close to the bottom, and I did whatever work came my way."

"Did your family have a farm or ranch?"

"Um, no, my father left, and then my mother did. I lived with a family that had a farm, so I worked for them and for other people as well, until I was able to go out on my own."

"And where was this?"

"In Ohio."

"That's a long ways. Did you come out here to work?"

"Yes, I did. I didn't have any family ties, and I didn't want to get stuck in a place where there wasn't much for me. I can always go back, of course, but I don't miss it so far."

"Do you like it here?"

"Of course I like it right here, because I met you. But I don't want to get ahead of myself." She left me to talk my way out of it, so I backed up and went forward. "I came out here to the West like a lot of young men do. I heard it was a place where a fellow could get a new start, and I heard also that it was a place where a man could find out if he had what it took."

She did not look straight at me as she said, "And what did you find out?"

"I haven't gotten the whole answer yet. This is indeed a proving ground, as they say. I think I've taken my buffets all right, but there are more hard, overbearing men than I expected."

"Oh, I know. I think they might be everywhere."

"I don't doubt it, but this seems to be an open range for some types. The foreman at the Clay Creek Ranch, for example. Paul Kelso."

"That one. Yes, he's a type. Medora has had to keep him at a distance."

"Then there's the other one, Holcomb. The one who told you to run along the other day."

"He seems very dangerous, very—"

"Sinister."

"That's it. They seem to live in a men's world, but they're more like animals—dogs or even wolves."

"They do seem dedicated to trying to prove who's at the top. Whether they're picking on youngsters like me, trying to be king stallion with other grown men, or—"

"Laying their eyes on women. Like Medora says, women in frontier towns have to put up with it with men from eighteen to eighty."

The back door of the café opened, and Eva's mother stepped out. I knew who she was, though I had not met her. She did not pay me a great deal of attention as she spoke to her daughter.

"When you finish with the potatoes, remember you have onions to cut up."

She had a clear voice with a slight accent I did not place. Perhaps it was the way the French-and-Indian people from the North talked, more noticeable in the woman who was named after the teal than in her daughter.

I also noticed her complexion, a little richer than Eva's. Seeing them together, I recalled the words "penny-skinned," which I had read in *The Last of the Mohicans* or some book like it.

When Priscilla went inside, Eva smiled at me and said, "Onions. Is that something else a wrangler does?"

"When we have 'em."

"Good. Because they make me cry."

I knew in what way she meant it, but her words still touched me in a soft spot. I recalled the way Holcomb had ordered her to go away and how she had vanished into the shadows, and I resented all men who hurt women and made them cry.

CHAPTER ELEVEN

Dunbar was smearing dark paste on his horse's hooves as he had done several days earlier. The shifting of hooves on the barn floor, the cackle of Carlyle's chickens, and the syllables Dunbar muttered to his horses combined in an undertone of tranquility. The flies had not let me sleep past dawn, but I did not have much to do. I sat against my saddle, or rather Carlyle's, and cleaned my fingernails as life took its slow pace.

Here in the barn where Bill Baker had filled the air with music, I could not drive away the tune about Lorena. I hummed other tunes, but "Lorena" kept coming back. With it came a sense of life I could not get over. Slavery had still been in practice some fifteen years before I was born, but I grew up in the North, and I had not known any people who had lived under that system. Maybe it was because of Bill Baker's singing, and maybe it was because the character in the song said it in such a simple and direct way, but I had been almost knocked over by the awareness that one man could own another as a slave, that he could sell the slave's sweetheart away to old Virginny, that he would have to read the letter, years later, telling of her death, and that the slave would take it all as part of his lot in life. I had read of similar events in *Uncle Tom's Cabin,* so I understood them, I might say, in an intellectual way. But the song, so understated and matter-of-fact, caught me on the emotional side, and the melody haunted me.

Dunbar finished his task, and we saddled up for our day's

ride. The cool of the morning still lay on the barnyard as we rode out. The day warmed up soon enough, however, as the heat of the sun reflected off of the dirt and the sparse grass. Dunbar was riding his blue roan, which stepped out at a brisk pace. My dark horse behaved well alongside the roan, except that a horsefly kept landing on various parts of the horse that were out of my hand's reach.

"Hang on," said Dunbar. He reined his horse, sagged back half a length, and swatted my horse's rump with his gloved hand.

My horse bolted but for only a few yards as I brought him under control.

"Got him," said Dunbar.

"Thanks." As we rode on, I realized I was breathing with my mouth open. I had to spit out a gnat. After that, I kept my mouth sealed. Sweat formed on my face and rolled down the inside of my shirt. This was the hot, dry part of the summer, and a fellow had to tolerate it.

We found Carlyle's cattle near a muddy water hole that was almost dried up. The count came out as always, and no animals had ailments, so we were done with our morning chore. Without a tree in sight, we drifted southward. Grasshoppers rose up in front of us and whirred away, while here and there a large black beetle labored in the dust. At times the grassland was teeming with life, from rabbits to grouse to antelope, but today was a day of insects.

Dunbar's voice broke the silence. "Over yonder is a little bluff. What say we shade up for a few minutes?"

"Sounds fine."

We angled east about half a mile until we came to the bluff, which rose about ten feet and still cast a bit of a shadow at this time of the morning. We dismounted and sat on a couple of mud boulders.

I said, "This reminds me of the place where Stanton's cow fell in the crevice. I would imagine they got her out."

"I suppose so, but there's no tellin' how hard they had to work."

"We could have asked Kelso." After a few seconds, I said, "What do you think he's up to?"

"No good, wherever he is."

"I don't miss him," I said. "If he wasn't picking on someone nearby, he was railing at someone far away. Not just the Mexicans and Indians and Negroes back home, but the Chinese in the gold country and the Swedes in the wheat country."

"He would probably dislike the pleasant Mrs. Carlyle if he had a chance."

"I don't recall that he ever mentioned her, but I wouldn't be surprised."

Dunbar brushed away a fly. "He would be a good one to belong to one of those secret groups, though I don't know of any around here."

"What kind would that be?"

"Well, the most obvious kind, and they're not all that secret, is the ones who hated abolitionists and now hate the free colored people."

"Are those the ones who lynch Negroes?"

"Some of them, yes. They form a vigilance group, and if they think they have cause, they take things into their own hands. Some of them terrorize black folks without much provocation." Dunbar had a faraway look in his eyes. "Then there's groups that do the opposite. They go after the first group, try to break up what they're doing. And on and on. Secret societies that hate Catholics. Others that want to take over the government. Anarchist groups that want to do away with government. Labor organizers who blow up company holdings. Strike breakers who cripple and kill union organizers. Even here you've got range

162

detectives, who are often little more than hired killers who do in little operators for a price. One or more men with money say that so-and-so is a rustler, and the man gets shot dead at his cabin door. Or they find him hangin' from a tree."

I said, "I knew about stock detectives and vigilance groups that lynched rustlers, or people accused of being rustlers, but I didn't know about secret societies. They sound worse."

"They're all bad, whether it's an organization with money and big plans or an individual who thinks he has the right to settle his hands on someone else's throat. Or put a bullet through him. In the case of individuals, the good thing is that sometimes they get paid back in kind. Of course, some don't. They die in comfort in old age. No justice in that."

While I thought I detected some amusement in the idea of antagonists waging war out of mutual malice, and while I was sure I detected contempt for the lone murderer who went free, I did not know what to make of his talk about secret societies. I could see that he disapproved of them, but I wondered if he had had any experience with them. Out here on the empty grassland, where my fancy could run free, I imagined a dangerous scenario in which Dunbar had been suspected as an infiltrator, burned in the hand, and expelled.

I said, "What about these secret societies? I suppose they have spies work their way inside."

"I imagine so. Just like detectives work their way into criminal groups. Rustlers, for example, or train robbers. And anti-union operatives work their way into labor organizations, which are sometimes pretty secret themselves."

"I wonder what they do when they catch a spy."

"If they've got any sense, they do away with 'em. As a practical matter, you know. I wouldn't want you to think I approved of it."

"What about defectors?" I asked. I was thinking about the

slave in *Uncle Tom's Cabin* who had been burned in the hand so that he could be identified if he tried to run away.

"The same, I would imagine. Just practical. Like walking the plank in the pirate stories."

I felt as if he had found me out, asking questions about real life as if it were an adventure story like *Treasure Island.* So I did not ask any more.

Our shade did not last long as the sun rose in the sky. We mounted up and rode onward. Still feeling sheepish for asking juvenile questions, I kept to myself. After a while, I surmised that we were headed toward Jack Brumley's place.

The sun had passed by the high point of the day when we rode into the yard. Aside from two horses raising a small cloud of dust in the corral, the place was quiet and still. Weeds around the house were turning dry, and the thistles along the barn had white blossom heads bursting into seed.

The front door opened. Jack Brumley appeared in the darkness of the doorway, his pale bald head in contrast with his weathered face. His eyes played over us.

"Afternoon," he said. "You can come in if you want."

We dismounted and tied our horses, then walked up the steps.

Jack stood back and held the door open. We walked through and turned to face him in the front room. I noticed his sagging gut, his rough hands with spots on the backs, and his tired, brown eyes with dark bags below.

"What's new?" he asked.

Dunbar said, "The latest news I know of is about Jane Lancaster, but you know about that. I saw you at the funeral."

"I know she died under suspicious circumstances, but I haven't heard anything about who was responsible."

"No one seems to be saying."

Jack had a cloudy look on his face. "How about a reason?"

"Same there. No one will come out and say anything."

Jack's eyes held on Dunbar. "What do you think?"

"I think someone thought she knew too much."

"That's as good a reason as any."

It struck me as curious that Jack did not ask any more, but I recalled that he did not seem to care much for Jane Lancaster, and as I would see in a minute, he was absorbed in his own problems.

"Would you like a drink?" he asked.

"Not for me," said Dunbar.

"No, thanks," I said.

"Well, I'm havin' somethin'. Come and sit down." He led the way to a wooden table, stained and varnished years earlier, with four spindle chairs. A whiskey bottle and a glass sat on the table in front of a chair that was pulled out. Jack took his seat. Dunbar sat across from him, and I sat at the end.

"Anything new with you?" said Dunbar.

"Nothin' of great importance. Rich Stanton came by yesterday."

"Oh?" said Dunbar.

Jack took a sip of whiskey. "He offered to buy my place."

Dunbar frowned. "I'm surprised he came around, after what his men did."

Jack's eyes moved back and forth between Dunbar and me. "He said he was sorry for what happened. Maybe he is. But like he said, he wasn't there. He didn't have anything to do with it."

"Do you believe that?"

"I don't know."

"You don't think he was offering to buy your ranch as a way for making up for it, do you?"

"Not at the price he offered. Next to nothing."

"I wonder why he thought you would accept."

Jack ran his hand over his bare head. "He said I couldn't take care of it myself anymore, and he was doing me a favor."

"Do you believe that?"

"Maybe. I'm too old for all of this. And now that I've lost my son, not to mention my wife before that, none of it seems to matter very much. I'm not sure what I've got to live for, much less stay around this place. It's brought me nothing but heartache. But I guess I stay around because I don't know what else I would do." Jack gave a weary sigh. "Are you sure you don't want a drink?"

"No, thanks."

Jack took another sip of whiskey. "Come right down to it, I don't think he ever liked our kind, and he'd like to get rid of us once and for all."

"Could be," said Dunbar. "I know his foreman is that way. He was rude with Willard, and I hope you don't mind my saying this, but he made a comment about Willard's mother as well."

"About Louise."

"Yes."

"That's what Willard said. Son of a bitch likes to make slurs about anyone who isn't perfectly white. Well, I wouldn't be surprised if Stanton was the same way. Doesn't show it in public, is all."

"Good possibility. Do you think he disliked Louise?"

"I have no idea. He was busy with his own life at that time, as I recall. Gettin' married, buildin' a house."

"Do you think he was glad to see her gone?"

Jack gave a troubled look. "I don't know what for, unless, like I said, he wanted to see us all gone."

"I'm sorry. I guess I didn't say that very well. Someone who wasn't here at the time might find it too easy to say some things."

"It happened a long time ago."

Dunbar tipped his head to the side. "I imagine you remember everything about it, though."

"I can't remember things I didn't know."

"Of course not. But I'm sure you remember little things, such as what she was wearing the last time you saw her."

Jack's eyes opened, though the expression was still dull. "As a matter of fact, I do. It was a dress she wore around the house. But she didn't take it with her."

"Oh, I see. She would have changed into something else. Do you happen to remember what that would be?"

"Like I said, it was a long time ago. She wouldn't be wearing it now. But based on what was missing from her things, I would say she was wearing a lavender-colored dress and a pair of golden earrings." Jack frowned. "Do you think you saw her somewhere?"

"I doubt it."

"You would have been pretty young, wherever you were."

"A little younger than Whit here. But I find all these things interesting. You know, the details."

"She was a woman that if you saw her, you would remember."

Dunbar did not answer. I had the feeling that he did not want to raise Jack's hope.

Jack put both hands on the table. "I'll show you a picture of her. Wait here." He pushed himself up from his chair and left the table.

He came back a minute later and set a photograph in front of Dunbar. The picture was mounted on a pasteboard mat and frame. Dunbar picked it up, looked at it for a long moment, and handed it to me.

The image was not sharp, but it drew my full attention. In its dusky quality, it showed a woman with large, dark eyes, a smoky complexion, full lips, wavy dark hair that covered her ears and was tied loosely in back, and a dark, high-collared dress with rounded shoulders.

I stopped breathing for a second, and a wave of dizziness

passed over me. As I regained my senses, I held the picture tight so that my hands would not be seen shaking. I took a couple of steady breaths and focused again on the photograph. Some essence of it struck deep into me. Louise Brumley did not look anything like my mother, but for a moment I had the illusion that Willard and I were the same person, that our mothers were the same person, and that I was communing with a spirit I would never see again.

My breathing was even and my hands were steady as I handed the photograph to Jack. "Very nice," I said.

Jack's eyes were misty. He said, "She was a beautiful woman. I was proud of her."

In another setting, this scene of a half-drunk man, an old photograph of a woman long gone, a dimly lit room, and the odor of whiskey would have struck me as maudlin. But having seen the image of Louise, I could not help having to blink away a few tears myself.

Jack turned to Dunbar. "What do you think? Does she look familiar? Do you think you've ever seen her?"

Dunbar shook his head. "I'm afraid not. But I agree with you. She's a beautiful woman."

In Carlyle's barn that evening, Dunbar and I enjoyed a supper of cut-up ham cooked in a dish with onions and potatoes.

"There's something about a woman's touch," said Dunbar. "You or I could make up an acceptable dish with these main ingredients, but a woman goes to more trouble. She puts in spices that you and I wouldn't have on hand, and unless I miss my guess, there's some milk in this as well."

"I think there might be some butter," I said.

"I believe you're right."

After we finished our main course, Carlyle showed up with two generous slices of chocolate cake.

"Whoa," said Dunbar. "This is more than we deserve."

"Elsie's glad for the opportunity. She loves to cook these things, and I can eat only so much."

"We're glad to help. Please send her our compliments."

"I will."

When Carlyle had taken away the last of the dishes, Dunbar rummaged through his gear and took out a sharpening stone that was seated in a wooden case. From his pocket he drew out a pen knife that I had not seen before. With a few drops of oil from a small can, he slicked the stone and then went about sharpening his knife. When the edge met the approval of his thumb, he put away the oil and the stone. I wondered if he was going to use the knife for something, like cutting leather to repair some piece of gear. To my surprise, he took out a pencil and sharpened it with a dozen short strokes, drawing the blade toward him and shaving the wood in thin curls.

He must have noticed my surprise, for he said, "Every good puncher should have a tally book, and of course something he can use to write in it. Not only do you keep track of cattle and brands and such, but you can jot down other things as well and not burden yourself with remembering. When you first start out, you remember everything, but as time goes on, you realize you're better off not trying to carry it all in your head. So you write down things."

"For example?"

"Well, you don't have to write down things you're not likely to forget, like the name of Rutledge's dead wife, or things you're not likely to need again, like the name of Lennox's dead brother. But you might note other things, like the name of the photographer who took Mrs. Brumley's picture or the brand of Mr. Stanton's saddle."

"Why would you write those things down?"

"I wouldn't write them, either, as I'm not likely to forget

169

them, especially after talking about them. But one reason in general is to teach you to notice things like that. Mrs. Brumley's picture was taken in Colorado Springs, and Mr. Stanton's saddle was made in Cheyenne, Wyoming, by F.A. Meanea. He probably bought it right out of the shop."

"Do you think Jack Brumley met Louise in Colorado Springs?"

"I have no idea at the moment. But if it ever mattered, it would be a question to ask. More important, as far as the photographer's name goes, is that he would be the person to ask if you needed to know the date of the picture—and if Jack couldn't tell you."

"Interesting information, Colorado Springs. It gives you the feeling that you know the person a little better."

"It does. Every little bit helps."

"I must say that when I saw the picture, I had the sense that now I knew her. In a way I felt as if I recognized her, but I realized it was a quality she had, or that I saw in her. She reminded me of my own mother, though she was much prettier. Like an angel." I almost said, "A dark angel," but it didn't sound right.

"She had a distinct beauty about her, that's for sure."

"As I recall, both Willard and Jack said she was Creole."

"That's true. You know, some very beautiful women have come from mixed backgrounds—a cross in the blood, as some people put it."

"Like Cora," I said. This time I spoke as the idea hit me.

"Cora?"

"Yes. I guess I blurted it out. She's the dark girl in *The Last of the Mohicans*."

"Oh, yes. That one. She's beautiful in that story. Her darkness came by way of the West Indies, I believe. Too bad she had to die. Seems kind of unfair. But that's Cooper for you. Sort of a blue blood in spite of himself. But back to the topic—yes, Mrs. Brumley's is a striking photograph."

"She wouldn't have been very old in that picture," I ventured.

"No, and as far as that goes, she wouldn't have been much older when she went missing. She would have been less than thirty when Jack Brumley was in love with her and Jane Lancaster was her friend."

It took me a moment to adjust my chronology. From all of the earlier conversations and references to her, I had formed an idea of Louise Brumley as the mother of a full-grown man and therefore somewhat matronly. But given the last time she was seen in town, and the natural way with which Dunbar spoke of her in the past tense, I began to accept the possibility that Louise Brumley had been a beautiful young woman when the end came for her.

CHAPTER TWELVE

Dunbar regarded the serving of apple pie with an expression of appreciation as he cut the tip of the triangle with his fork. Although at moments like this he gave the appearance of having nothing else to do in his stay at Dry Camp, I sensed that he was working on a purpose, or, to put it in stronger terms, on a mission. He had told me on an earlier occasion that he followed his curiosity, but I did not think his interest was that casual. Furthermore, I thought he had arrived at his conclusions and was waiting for something.

Meanwhile, he sampled the pie and appraised it with leisure. Medora stood by, her wavy dark hair and rich complexion making a handsome contrast with her white blouse.

"This is very good," he said. "Ideal. As if there existed a perfect apple pie, made in a celestial bakery, and it materialized here. And yet this was probably made by one person, here in your kitchen."

"It was," said Medora, with a half-smile as she brushed back her hair with her hand.

I admired her restraint in not telling him who made the pie.

Dunbar ate a second bite before he spoke again. "You know we came straight here. Didn't stop at the barber shop, the saloon, or the post office to catch up on the latest news. Of course, we wonder if there is any."

"Arrivals and departures," said Medora. She set her lips in a

172

way that I thought was pretty, and I was sure Dunbar thought so, too.

"Sounds interesting," he said as he gazed at her.

"The deputy arrived."

The expression on Dunbar's face opened. "That's good. One might have wondered."

"He put up at the Waverly Hotel, of course. I don't know that he has done anything yet."

"And the departures? Or was there something else in the arrivals category?"

Medora pursed her lips. "No, that was it for arrivals. Just one. The departures were plural."

Dunbar nodded for her to go ahead.

"Mr. Stanton has taken his wife and daughters to the train so that they can go to Glenwood Springs."

"That's a resort, isn't it?"

"Yes, in Colorado. People go there to enjoy the cooler mountain climate and to try the waters." Medora smiled, and her dark eyes had a shine of amusement. "They left on the stage that brought the deputy. But as you know, two things happening in sequence does not mean that the first event caused the second."

Dunbar smiled in return. "Makes for good humor, sometimes. For example, when you consider that I recited a poem at the Fourth of July picnic and we had three inches of rain that night, you have some idea of my powers of elocution."

Medora laughed. "You have your share of eloquence."

"Inspired by the pie." After a few seconds, he said, "Interesting that Stanton left town. Do you know him at all?"

Medora glanced around, as if to be sure there were no other customers in the café. All of the tables had been cleared, and sounds from the kitchen suggested that the employees were busy washing the dishes, pots, and pans from breakfast. Medora brought her eyes back to Dunbar and spoke in a lowered voice. "He has come in here a few times. I haven't crossed paths with him anywhere else."

Dunbar said, "I know him even less, I'm sure. He makes me curious, though. He seems to be a man of some status, what with a ranch, a house in town, business dealings with his father-in-law, and his association with other cattlemen. And yet his foreman and his new hired man are so—"

"Uncouth."

"That's a good word for them."

Medora's eyebrows flickered. "It's based mainly on my acquaintance with Mr. Kelso, plus what I've heard about the other one, Holcomb."

Dunbar said, "In my view, the word applies to both of them in various ways. One thing that makes me curious is the question of whether Stanton tolerates their habits or whether he goes along with them to some extent."

"Well, he hasn't fired them for what they've done."

"I'm thinking in particular about Kelso and his attitude toward people who aren't as white as he is. He can be quite ugly about it."

Medora stood with her hands together at her waist. "It doesn't surprise me."

"So what I'm wondering is . . . whether Stanton has some kinship with that kind of attitude."

Medora raised her eyebrows in a skeptical expression. "With the exception of the ranch, which I know nothing about, he lives a rather consistent life. As you described his status a minute ago, he lives with and associates with well-to-do, typical white Americans."

"Yes, but I haven't gotten a glimpse of how he might regard people who aren't of his class."

Medora looked at me. "What do you think? You worked for him."

I was caught off guard. "I don't know. If he ever had anything against Willard, he hid it very well. Kelso didn't. That is, he didn't hide it at all."

Medora turned her eyes toward Dunbar and spoke in a low, confidential tone. "Here's what I think, or rather what I think I've noticed. I believe Mr. Stanton is not always good at hiding what he feels. He can look at me and be civil, even as he has his ulterior thoughts. But I've also seen the looks he has given Eva's mother. As if she were another species." Medora hesitated. "Fit for breeding. I know that sounds coarse, but it's the way I've seen him when he was looking in another direction and didn't know I was watching. I think he sizes up every woman he sees, even the younger ones, and if a woman has a bit of color— well, I've already said it." Medora's eyes moved to me and back to Dunbar. "I apologize for speaking in blunt terms about it. But you asked me, and that's my impression. A woman can sense things that another man might not."

"I believe that," said Dunbar, "and I appreciate your discretion."

Medora tossed a glance again to either side, and this time I realized that she might be confirming that Eva and her mother were not within easy listening distance. She raised her head and said, "I'm sorry if I've seemed willing to malign him, but I don't like some things I've seen."

"It's all right," said Dunbar. "I think we're of a shared mind." He looked downward and cut into the pie again with his fork.

Medora nodded in a thoughtful expression.

In that moment, I could feel the truth of what Dunbar said. He and Medora were kindred spirits including me in their company. My head was swimming in mild undulations between the dead-serious things that had happened in Dry Camp and the ethereal world of higher principles, where he and she met. I found myself believing in the celestial bakery, and in my exalted state, I thought Eva would have, too, if she had been there with us.

The sun at late morning reflected off the wooden buildings, and heat rose from the street. Dunbar and I walked the three blocks to the Waverly Hotel, leading our horses. We tied up at the hitching rail, walked past the multicolored petunias, and climbed the plank steps into shadow.

Dunbar pushed upon the door with the red lettering and the frosted glass, and we passed through. The bell jingled as usual, and the rug muffled our steps as we entered the lobby. Gilbert Rutledge did not appear from behind the reception desk, but within a few seconds he emerged from the dining area. He was wearing a suit of gun-metal blue, which brought out his silver hair and blue eyes. He was clean-shaven as always.

"Gentlemen," he said. "How do you do?"

"Well enough," said Dunbar.

Rutledge glanced at each of us. "Borne on a fair wind, I hope."

Dunbar said, "Not an ill one, at least." He waited for a couple of seconds and continued. "I understand the deputy has come to town."

"He has, thanks in part to your efforts."

"Quite all right. I'd like to ask, if I might, whether he has found out anything."

Rutledge did not answer but waited for Dunbar to say more.

"About the death of Mrs. Lancaster."

"Of course." Rutledge set his lips closed and then spoke again. "He just came in on the last stage. We got him settled into a room, and now he's having something to eat. He missed breakfast, so we're serving him an early noon dinner."

Dunbar said, "I didn't mean to hurry anyone. I'm glad he's here. The woman deserves some justice."

"Of course she does. As we said before, every little thing matters. Even if, well, to put it frankly, the loss is not all that great."

I was appalled, and I wondered if I had heard him right.

Dunbar frowned. "I'm not sure I catch your meaning."

Rutledge gave a small wave of the hand. "No great matter. Just my impression."

"Oh. I thought she had been of service to this town."

"Well, yes. She helped bring a few babies into the world, that's true. But if the stories I heard had any truth to them, she didn't always help in that way."

Dunbar bore down with his dark eyes. "I'm afraid I don't follow you again."

Rutledge glanced around and came back to Dunbar. "These things are rather disagreeable to talk about, but I've understood that on more than one occasion she helped a woman with something she didn't want to have."

A feeling of dread crept through me. At that point in my life I had heard a few references to women getting rid of babies before and after they were born, and it all seemed hideous and foreign to me. I did not know how much of it I wanted to hear now.

Dunbar spoke. "People say a lot of things."

"They do. And I don't know how true they are. But I think there might be some basis to them." Rutledge paused, as if he was weighing how much more to say. "Again, I don't know. But there's another thing." He moistened his lips. "I don't know of any evidence that she had ever been married. She didn't seem to have much use for men, at least in that way. Who knows what her motives were."

I was almost overwhelmed by the innuendo, tossed out as the three of us stood in the middle of the reception area. Dunbar seemed to be measuring his own response.

He said, "To borrow wisdom from the Reverend Mansfield, it's not for us to judge."

Rutledge, in turn, seemed to land right away on his own level of proper conduct. "By all means," he said. "Let the good woman rest in peace." Then, with a new breath, as if he had not even mentioned Mrs. Lancaster, he said, "I wish you men would give another thought to working with me on the Madeleine project."

Dunbar did not blink as he said, "We haven't dismissed the idea."

"Oh, good."

Rutledge looked at me, and I nodded, as if Dunbar and I had been in agreement. In truth, I was not as surprised as I might have been, for my memory had kept a residue of Dunbar's bantering conversation with Pat Hendy.

Dunbar spoke again. "As far as that goes, we have a little time, either today or tomorrow, to go down there and look at it."

"Really?"

"Just to take a look. I can't guarantee we'll work on it because we don't know what else might come up."

"Of course. But there's nothing like taking a look at something for yourself."

"I agree."

"I'll give you directions, then. Nothing complicated."

Dunbar nodded.

Rutledge walked around the end of the reception desk and took his place behind it. I thought he was going to write out directions, but he raised his brass letter knife and began to draw an invisible map on the top of the counter.

"Take the main road south of town. A few miles out, it veers to the southwest and then holds south again. You go over a good-sized ridge, mostly grass and sagebrush. Off to the west, where the land sweeps up and around to the mountains, you'll see trees. Mostly cedar. But you stick to the main road, and the country levels out to the south. By and by you'll come to a road that goes east and west. The road you're on will go past that road into rougher country, but you don't follow it anymore." Rutledge continued to trace the map with the knife. "At the crossroads, you turn left and go east about a mile. Right along that roadway, you'll find our section of land. One square mile with a pile of rocks on each corner for a marker."

Dunbar said, "Is there anything else around there? Any settlements or ranch houses?"

Rutledge tapped the tip of the knife on the countertop. "Nothing. That's why it's a good location. The road that goes east and west is the route that the railroad is going to take, only a half mile or so to the south. There's nothing on that route for twenty miles in either direction, so when we put in our town, it'll be a natural stop. You'll see the potential when you get there."

"Sounds easy enough to find."

"You can't miss it." Rutledge's gaze lingered over both of us. "When do you think you'll go?"

Dunbar said, "Not sure yet. If we don't go today, it'll be tomorrow."

"Anytime's good enough. When you get back, we can talk about it some more." Rutledge smiled and gave a small nod of assurance.

"You bet," said Dunbar. He tipped his head as he looked at me. "Ready?"

We shook hands with Rutledge and walked out into the bright, hot day. As we gathered our reins, I spoke to Dunbar in a low voice.

"How strong is your interest in this project?"

"Mild at best," he said. "I'm more interested in knowing

what Stanton is up to. Whatever it is, I don't think Rutledge is in cahoots with him."

"I don't follow you. They're partners on this plan to build a town."

"Oh, that. Yes, they are. Or at least I believe they are. But as for whatever is going on in this town, I don't think Rutledge has a hand in it. If he did, he would want to know more about our coming and going."

I pondered that idea for a moment and said, "So we're going to go look at this town site just out of curiosity?"

"You might say that. Sometimes when you look at a place, it says something to you. I don't expect it in this case, but we'll see."

We rode south that afternoon and arrived at the site without incident in about three hours. We had ridden through the heat of the day but had taken it slow. Following the road eastward from the crossroads, we came upon the town site and faced it, looking north.

The country spread out in an unbroken expanse of sagebrush, grass, and dirt. From our vantage point I could see the foot-high pyramid of small rocks we had gone past, but the other three markers were not visible. I knew that a section consisted of a square mile, with six hundred forty acres, but I could not tell where the boundaries lay. The tract was common and not distinguished in any way from the surrounding thousands of acres.

We rode around the perimeter, from one little pile of rocks to the next, and came back to our original point of observation.

"There's not much here," said Dunbar. "You can see the plan, though. These fellows take an inexpensive piece of land and in effect create more property by cutting it into pieces, subdividing and then subdividing again, the way speculators do."

"Like you said before, selling dirt."

"It all depends on water. If they can't get a well drilled, they can't sell lots. And the train wouldn't stop here." Dunbar glanced across the open country to the east. "And who knows how certain it is that the railroad will even come through." He rested his gloved hands on his saddle horn and resumed his study of the town site. "I'd say it'll be a while before Pat Hendy or anyone else is in here scraping streets. This is just an idea, and maybe a sentimental one."

I recalled that earlier comment of his, about selling dirt, when he also referred to this project as a memorial to a dead wife. I said, "I can just as easily picture a cemetery as a town taking shape here."

Dunbar smiled. "You can divide it into more lots that way. Of course, to have a cemetery, you need a town or a city." His eyes roved over the sagebrush and dirt. "I see what you mean, though."

After a quiet moment, I said, "Well, we've had a look at the place. Has it said anything to you?"

He shook his head. "No, everything seems to be on the surface. Nothing deeper that I can get a sense of."

Back in the town of Dry Camp, we arranged to spend the night at Hunton's lodging house. After a day of thin shadows and broad, sparse country, Hunton's furnishings seemed close and cramped. We sat at his table in the heavy atmosphere of the kitchen, where he had cooked up a skillet of hash and now reheated it. The smell of friend onions hung on the air, and the food came out scorched and greasy. Hunton used the same flapper he had brandished on that earlier occasion when he served flapjacks, and now he whacked it on the lip of the skillet to dislodge the fragments of food.

After forcing myself to eat a couple of bites of hash, I saw that Hunton had traded his flapper for a fly swatter. I kept one eye on him from then on, as I thought he might be the type who would not notice if a fly fell in amongst the burnt onions.

Hunton turned out to be quick at swatting flies and scrupulous about brushing them off the counter and table so that they fell on the floor. As on our two earlier stays, I tried to imagine this man with glassy eyes, a swollen nose, and a protruding stomach as a younger, leaner man, in buckskins and a coonskin cap like Daniel Boone or Davy Crockett, fighting Indians with rifle and tomahawk. I tried to picture his two wives, and they did not come out as pretty as Cora and her fair sister, Alice, in *The Last of the Mohicans*. I reminded myself that he had had these wives in sequence, not side by side, and probably a good while after his flamboyant youth. I imagined them as plain-looking women who did not hold up well in the harshness of frontier life. Still, two women had seen fit to marry him, and incongruous though it seemed, he had had as many wives as Jack Brumley and Gilbert Rutledge put together.

Dunbar had not been putting away the hash any faster than I was. He rested his fork and said, in a casual tone, "I saw you at Mrs. Lancaster's funeral. Did you know her very well?"

Hunton answered with an odd quack in his voice. "Not particularly." His stomach rose and fell. "A few of us had something in common, though. We were what you might call underdogs."

"As opposed to—?"

"The Rutledges and Stantons and those who make up to them."

"Is there some kind of an ongoing battle?"

Hunton's voice quacked again. "Not really. But some people run things and grab all the opportunities, and some of us are kept on the outside. It's not an easy living, especially when you're made to feel second class."

"How much opportunity is there in this town?"

"Not much. But people come in from the ranches, and some travelers do pass through."

Dunbar spoke without looking up. "And yet Mr. Rutledge wants to build another town."

"I've heard of that." Hunton's clipped words brought out his accent.

"Do you think it's just a land scheme?"

Hunton swatted a fly on the countertop and brushed it onto the floor. "I have no idea. I don't keep up with him."

Dunbar brushed his mustache. "Did you know his wife?"

"Hah. I barely knew my own."

"He wants to name his town after her, you know."

"I've heard that, too."

Dunbar said, "Well, I'll make no secret of it. Mr. Rutledge has offered us work on the project. But I don't know how far away it is."

"I couldn't tell you."

"I couldn't, either. We went down there today to take a look, and all we saw was bare land."

"That makes sense."

Dunbar had taken up his fork, but he held it in pause as he looked at Hunton. "In what way?"

"I heard someone was askin' where you two went."

"Oh. The deputy?"

"No. I heard he was in town, but I don't know if he went out."

I thought Hunton was being coy with us, and Dunbar did not seem to be in a hurry to play along. So I said, "Who was looking for us?"

Hunton's peculiar accent came out again as he said, in his

matter-of-fact way, "Well, it wasn't a pretty girl, I'll tell you that. It was Paul Kelso."

Dunbar gave a short laugh and said, "There aren't many secrets in this town. Kelso could have asked Mr. Rutledge, but I don't think they're on that good of terms."

Hunton said, "Kelso doesn't spend much time at the Waverly."

Dunbar poked at his hash. "Even less when the deputy's there, I imagine. But sooner or later the deputy will have questions of his own."

CHAPTER THIRTEEN

A confusion of sounds woke me. From somewhere in town, outside the open window of our room in the lodging house, shouting voices mixed with the din of someone beating on a washtub. Inside the dark room, Dunbar was standing up, stamping into his boots and buckling on his gunbelt.

I threw off the covers and sat up on the side of the bed. "What's going on?" I asked.

"Sounds like a fire."

I shook my head. I had been dreaming something that I could not remember, and the sounds from outside had entered my dream. Now things were separating, and the noises from outside were beginning to make sense. The beating on the washtub continued, and a couple of voices alternated in calling out the alarm.

"I'm going out to help," said Dunbar.

My head was clearing. "I'll be along in a minute," I said.

Dunbar's steps sounded in the hallway as I gathered my clothes and began dressing. More voices were clamoring in the street, and the odor of smoke drifted in through the window.

My mouth had a dry, stale taste as I made my way down the hallway, but my eyes were open and my mind was clear as I stepped out into the night. Human forms moved in the darkness. A block away, beyond the main street, firelight gleamed. I imagined someone's house had caught fire, so the blaze was not as big as it would be if one of the businesses had gone up.

A lantern appeared, and I saw that some of the townspeople had formed a bucket brigade. With the well three blocks to the west and the fire a block to the north, the people were spread out, so each person had to carry a bucket of water some twenty yards. That was the movement I had first seen.

I took my place in the line between two men I did not know. I moved one way and the other as the men called for me to relay a full bucket or an empty one. After a few minutes, I heard Gilbert Rutledge's voice as he moved along the line from the direction of the fire. He was not carrying buckets but was speaking to each person.

When he came to me, he said, "We've got it confined to just one house. It's not going anywhere else. Just keep moving the water, and we'll have it under control in a little while."

The man on my left appeared with a full bucket. As he handed it to me, he spoke to Rutledge. "Whose house is it?"

"Old Lennox. The drunk."

"Was he in it?"

"We don't know yet. If he was, it doesn't look good for him."

With the full bucket at my side, I ran in a crouch in the direction of the blaze. I tried to concentrate on the work of carrying the bucket even and smooth, not letting it slosh, and handing it off to the next man, but I could not keep my thoughts from racing. It was happening again. Someone else had been killed. Another person who either knew too much or said too much.

The buckets kept moving, one way and the other, full and empty. I tried to figure how many buckets were in use, but I could not keep track. I recognized each one when it came back empty, but the buckets came at irregular intervals in both directions, and it seemed to me that the sequence did not stay the same. There were a couple of wooden buckets with rope handles, at least three tin pails of varying thicknesses, two or three galvanized buckets, and one that was made of an alloy like brass but of a dull, grayish hue.

The firelight dimmed, and the heavier, clotting smell of doused burning wood hung on the air. Word came along with a pair of empty buckets.

"That's enough."

We passed the remaining full buckets to the site of the dying fire. One by one, the men in the brigade drifted to the scene. Half a dozen lanterns shed light, and a crowd formed. Other onlookers gathered. Voices muttered. "Was the old man dead?" "He must have been smoking and he fell asleep." "Just lucky that no one else's house caught fire." "Too bad about the old man, but he drank a lot."

The talk went on that way for a few minutes, and then it gave way to expressions of surprise and a gradual hush. A couple of men raised their lanterns higher and showed light beyond the edge of the crowd. Facing the crowd as it turned was Ambrose Lennox, unkempt as usual but without a smudge.

"What the hell's going on?" he asked.

Gilbert Rutledge stepped forward. "Thank God you're alive. We were afraid you'd been burned to death."

The old man's face hardened. "And why 'n the hell would that be?"

"Well, your house just burned to the ground."

"I can see that, but I want to know why."

Rutledge shook his head. "God only knows. We assumed you were here and might have been careless with something."

"Careless, my ass. I wasn't here. I was at Jane Lancaster's, keeping an eye on things there."

Rutledge frowned. "What were you doing that for?"

Lennox cast a glance around the crowd. "No one else is."

"I'll have you know there's a deputy in town, looking into matters related to recent deaths."

"A fine lot of good he's doing. Where is he? Sleeping in your fine hotel?"

A voice came from the back of the crowd. "I'm right here."

The crowd parted, and a man walked forward. He was of average height and was dressed in an everyday outfit of a hat, a tan canvas shirt, a leather vest, denim trousers, a gunbelt, and scuffed brown boots. He had narrow shoulders and a sparse mustache, and if it were not for the star that shone in the lamplight, an average observer would not have picked him out for a lawman.

He came to a stop next to Rutledge and rested his thumb on his gunbelt. His narrow eyes held on Lennox and relaxed. "I'm Deputy Nance of the Albany County Sheriff's office. If you have any complaints, I'll be glad to listen to them."

Lennox's head made a slow turn, like that of an old dog. "I'd like to know who burned down my house because I sure as hell didn't."

Deputy Nance did not blink. "We don't know yet if anyone burned it down. But I can begin looking for evidence when I've got some daylight. I'll tell you right now, though, that it's not the first thing on my list."

"You can be sure I'll have questions later, then."

"I'll be expecting them." Deputy Nance made a half-turn and spoke to the crowd. "I think we're done for the night. Thanks to everyone who helped, and I'd appreciate it if everyone would stay clear of this scene until I've had a chance to look it over."

Lennox said, "I suppose that means me, too."

"I'm sure there are things you'd like to check on, and I can't keep you from it, but it would be better to stay away and not disturb anything. If you don't mind."

Lennox's eyes blazed. "If I don't mind? Some son of a bitch burns my house down, probably with the intention of finishing me off with it, and I'm supposed to stand by and not mind?"

The deputy took in a short breath. "We don't know what or how much was intended, but we'll try to find out."

I felt sympathy for Lennox as he stood there flat-footed, a grubby old man with bleary eyes, thin hair, and sagging clothes—a man whose habits had left him little to live on even in good times and who now had nothing.

But Lennox was not looking for sympathy. In a mocking tone, he said, "We'll try to find out. Well, let me tell you. This thing started with the death of an old man, for no good reason, and someone tried to end it that way. This was no accident. They say some people will burn a house to kill a rat. Seems to me that others will burn a house and try to make it seem like the rat did it himself. They came close, and I'm just lucky I kept myself out of the way."

Deputy Nance showed no expression as he said, "I'll look into it. But like I say, it won't be the first thing I do tomorrow."

Hunton banged on our door at what seemed like an early hour, but when I opened my eyes, the gray of morning was visible outside the window.

"We'll be right there," I said. As I rolled out and sat up, I saw that Dunbar was gone. I got dressed, washed my face in the basin at the head of the hallway, and made my way to the kitchen and eating area.

The smell of fried food scared me, as I feared that Hunton was going to serve up more of last night's hash. The sight of a skillet of sliced potatoes settled my fears, and I took a seat.

Hunton looked down his large nose at me. "Where's your friend?"

"I don't know."

"I heard him go out."

"I imagine he'll be back before long."

Hunton began laying slices of bacon in a second skillet. "Too bad about the old man's house burning down."

"Yes, it is."

His accent was audible as he said, "Who knows if anyone will do anything about it."

"I hope so."

Hunton stared at me with his glassy eyes. "You know, I've heard people say that all of this funny stuff started when your friend came to town."

"That doesn't mean he caused any of it."

"I didn't say that. I was going to make another point. I think some people say things to try to divert attention. As for me, I don't think your friend is the kind to go around tormenting old people."

"Or colored people."

"That, too." Hunton resumed laying bacon in the skillet.

The sound of the front door opening broke off our conversation. I recognized Dunbar's footsteps, and in a minute he made his appearance.

"Good morning," he said. He took off his hat and sat across the table from me.

"Busy night," said Hunton as he wiped his hands on a towel.

"Yes, it was."

"I heard you go out again, just before dawn."

"Sometimes it's hard to sleep."

"I hope you weren't looking for your notebook."

Dunbar's eyes opened wide. "Why?"

"I found it where you dropped it in the hallway." Hunton reached inside his vest and brought out Dunbar's tally book. He handed it across the table.

"Thanks."

"Think nothin' of it." Hunton seemed to enjoy this tiny bit of superiority. He poked at the bacon with his flapper, and without looking at either of us, he said, "You'd think it might be risky, leavin' a notebook layin' around, but I noticed it doesn't have anything written in it."

Dunbar said, "It's my tally book. I'm between roundups."

"I figured it was yours, though. I'd seen something like it in your shirt pocket. Is that why you went out this morning, to look for it?"

"I went out because I couldn't sleep."

"I'm the same way," said Hunton. "I sleep with one eye open. Once you've been attacked by Indians, you never forget it." He poked again at the bacon, which was beginning to bubble and hiss. I thought he eyed it with caution, as if the stovetop was a hostile landscape with Apache smoke signals on the rise.

"What kind of Indians did you fight?" I asked.

"The worst kind," he answered. "The kind that would cut your heart out before your very eyes, or hang you upside-down in a pit of rattlesnakes."

"You must have had some narrow escapes."

"I should say I did. But I don't like to talk about it." He used the flapper to lift a slice of bacon. "Figure this," he said. "The Waverly Hotel buys its bacon and potatoes in the same place as I do. But you'd never know it, to compare the prices between the two places."

The idea of Hunton in a broad set of buckskins, trussed up and hanging upside-down in a snake pit, was amusing to consider, but when Dunbar and I stepped out into the street, the serious world came back. The stale odor of charred lumber hung in the air. The path of the bucket brigade was visible, as the splashes of water had not dried yet, and the hundreds of footprints in the dirt had not been ridden over.

I wondered how Ambrose Lennox was holding up. He must have found it unnerving to have someone make such a move against him. I reflected on his remark that he had kept himself out of the way. Even if he was an old drunk, he was not a fool.

"Do you think we should go check on Lennox?" I asked.

"I dropped in on him earlier. He's all right."

"Were you out making the rounds?"

"Something like that. I was wondering if anyone would be tampering with the burned ruins, but not a person was stirring in the whole town."

I pictured Stanton's house, still and quiet. "Has it occurred to you," I asked, "that this was a convenient time for Stanton to be away?"

"Yes, it has. And I haven't forgotten that Kelso was asking about our whereabouts yesterday afternoon."

We were walking in the direction of the livery stable and the town well. I said, "What's our plan for today? Do we go back out to Carlyle's?"

"Not right away. I'm waiting to hear about something."

"Oh. I thought we were headed toward the livery stable."

"We are. I wanted to check on our horses, and I'm curious as to whether anyone has come or gone."

The main street lay in full sunlight, and signs of life appeared along the sidewalks. Across the street, a barrel with new mops and brooms stood beside the open door of the general store. The butcher had set out his folding sign. On our side of the street, the post office was open. As we walked by, I glanced inside and saw an angular man leaning with his elbow on the counter and with his jaw on the heel of his hand. Two doors down, the barber was shaving a man who lay back with his feet pointing up. On the next block, across the street, the Waverly Hotel came into view, shining in its coat of grayish-blue with red trim. At its base, the bed of white, red, purple, and pink petunias smiled in the sun.

Inside the livery stable, my eyes adjusted to the shadows. The stable man met us with a pitchfork held upright.

"Come for your horses?"

"Not quite yet," said Dunbar. "We just dropped in to check."

"Uh-huh."

"Has anyone new come in?"

"If you mean travelers, no. Not since yesterday when the deppity came in on the stage."

"I see. Do you know if he's been up and around today?"

"He left early."

"On horseback?"

"Yes. He got a horse from me. Said he was going out to talk to Jack Brumley." The stable man's thin eyebrows and pale blue eyes showed little expression. When Dunbar did not say anything in response, the man said, "That's the law for you. A woman gets killed in town, a man's house burns down, and the deppity goes out to the country to look for clues."

"Maybe he knows his business," said Dunbar.

"You hope so. But the way he goes about it, you'd think he was from the city. Then again, I guess he is. Laramie City."

"There are worse places."

"Oh, yeah. I've been to some."

Dunbar thanked him, and we left. When we were out on the street again and headed toward the center of town, Dunbar shook his head and gave a slight frown. "I don't know why the fellow wants to make fun of Laramie. They've got a good prison there, and a university." He smiled. "Sort of like the two gates in one of those old Greek stories, or the separate paths that lead to destruction and salvation." He sniffed. "Lots of information in those two places, depending on what you want to know."

"I haven't been there, but it's a place I'd like to go."

"Best way to do it is under your own volition."

I gave him a sideways glance. "Have you gone there other-wise?"

"Oh, no. But I've had occasion to interview a couple of men there."

"And the town itself?"

"It's on the railroad, so you get the good and the bad from that. Sometimes, though, you'll see one little thing that will stick in your mind, and you'll forever associate it with a place. Duluth, Minnesota, for example. One day I was walking across the street, and a man spit in the dirt right in front of me. Big ugly gob. I had to jump to miss it. So if I ever think of Duluth, I think of that. On the other hand, one day I was walking along the street in Laramie, and I saw a woman stepping up into a carriage. I didn't know the woman, and she didn't look like anyone rich or famous, but she was dressed in a respectable way—dark clothing and a hat. She gave me a glance and disappeared into the carriage. It was just that much, but it made me wonder about that woman and what her story was. I never saw her again, of course."

"What did she look like?"

"Dark hair, nice figure. Actually, she looked like Medora."

"Maybe it was."

Dunbar shook his head. "No. I asked her. Medora, that is. She said she's never been in Laramie."

"It would have been an interesting turn of fate if she had been."

"Wouldn't it, though?"

We were approaching the corner. I could see the café some two blocks ahead and across the street. I said, "Is that where we're headed right now?"

"Seems to be. I'm keeping pace with you, and your shoes seem to be taking us to Eva."

Inside the café, we dallied over coffee until the last of the breakfast customers had gone. Medora arrived at our table with the coffeepot. I noted her dark hair and nice figure, and I appreciated Dunbar's standards.

"You don't seem to be in a hurry," she said.

Dunbar smiled. "I hope you aren't, either. Do you have a minute or two to join us?"

"I suppose I could." She filled our two cups, set the coffeepot on the next table, and pulled a chair around. When she was seated, she said, "The fire last night is the news of the town."

"Not good at all," said Dunbar.

"At least there's a lawman in town. They say he went out to talk to Jack Brumley. You know, people haven't said much about what happened to Willard—not out loud, anyway. But it didn't take the deputy very long to find out about it and to wonder if it has any connection with these other . . . events. Mrs. Lancaster, and now this fire."

"Lennox made a comment last night, in front of everybody, that might have had some effect. He said all these troubles began with the death of an old man. Ross Guilford, of course. So I wouldn't be surprised if the deputy is asking about him as well."

Medora brushed back her hair. "It would be good if he did." Her eyes met Dunbar's. "You see a connection, I'm sure."

"Oh, yes. But I think it goes farther back than that."

"Really?" Medora's eyebrows tensed as she showed attention.

Dunbar spoke in a lower tone. "For me, it keeps leading back to Louise Brumley. That's why I went to see Jane Lancaster. I think she knew more than she told me, and I think someone wanted to quiet her."

Medora seemed to be reflecting.

"How well did you know Jane?" he asked.

"Not very well. Hardly at all."

"And Louise, of course, disappeared long before you ever came around."

"That's true. But you've got me to thinking about something

195

that Jane might have known." Medora shook her head. "I don't know."

"Go ahead," said Dunbar.

Medora had an uncomfortable expression on her face. "I don't know," she said again. "This is something I was told in confidence. But it might be pertinent." She had both hands on the table, and she held them so that the fingertips touched. She stared at the table, took a deep breath, and raised her eyebrows. She exhaled and looked at both of us.

"As you can imagine, in my time here, I have had attention from a variety of men, and I have heard some personal stories. One of those men was Jack Brumley. One night about a year ago, maybe less, he was softened by a few drinks and began to tell me about his lonely life. He talked about his wife leaving and how before that, they had not been happy. She had already had Willard when they met, which I think is not a great secret. But the sad part for Jack was that they didn't have any children of their own—that is, between the two of them. They tried, but they didn't have any luck." Medora looked at both of us and said, "I feel very bad telling this, but as I said, it might mean something."

"Go ahead," said Dunbar.

"Well, according to Jack, he felt that it was his fault and that it might have caused her to feel that she hadn't gotten enough out of life and that she might have gone somewhere else to seek it."

"Except that she left Willard behind."

"Yes. That makes no sense, unless she was infatuated with a man who wanted her by herself. I believe that's the commonly received idea."

"It's an easy one to settle on." Dunbar paused, as if he was measuring his own words. "Did Jack seem to think she was with child by someone else?"

"Oh, I don't know. He didn't say. I believe it hurt him to tell me as much as he did. But that's the way things go. I seem to attract men who have confessions to make."

Dunbar's eyes sparkled as he smiled and said, "Not always."

Medora suppressed a smile. "Be that as it may, I feel a bit guilty for having told someone else's story just now. But I did so because I thought it might help a person understand some aspect of the case better."

"It very well might," said Dunbar.

When we left the Deville Café, we took a short detour to pass by the remains of Ambrose Lennox's house. I expected to see a couple of curious onlookers, but the area around the small lot was deserted. The house had not burned to a neat bed of ash but had been reduced to a heap of charred boards and twisted metal objects, among them a pail, a wash basin, and a coal scuttle. A cast-iron stove sat upright in the ruins, but the pipe had fallen away. A stale odor emanated from the place, adding to a feeling of misery and waste.

Dunbar's gaze traveled around the site, and I wondered if this was another instance in which he thought a scene might tell him something. I was about to speak when I heard the steps of someone behind us. We both turned, and my pulse jumped when I recognized the features of Paul Kelso.

He stood with his head tipped back, his short-brimmed hat casting a light shadow on his eyes. His straight blond hair and flushed complexion caught the sun, and his upper lip area tightened over his teeth.

"Seems like you're always pokin' your nose into somethin'," he said. He laid his thumb on the ivory handle of his .45 pistol.

Dunbar said, "I could say the same for you. For a man who's supposed to be a ranch foreman, you spend a lot of time in town."

"I am a ranch foreman. If your memory works at all, you'll recall that I fired you." His eyes moved to me. "Both of you."

"Where's your boss?" said Dunbar.

Kelso's lip stayed tight over his teeth. "He's out of town. He left on family business."

I was surprised that Kelso gave a straight answer. Then it occurred to me that the deputy was out of town as well, and his absence might have given Kelso the encouragement to walk up on us.

Dunbar spoke again. "What do you know about this fire?"

Kelso sneered. "The old drunk was probably smoking when he passed out, then ran off to make it seem as if he didn't know anything about it."

"Maybe I missed my guess," said Dunbar.

"Wot's that?"

"I'd guess you tried to take care of him here. Same as he said to the deputy and everyone else. Don't know if you heard that."

Kelso spoke in a slow, deliberate tone. "It doesn't matter wot I heard."

"My guess is that if you'd known where he was, you would have done things differently."

Kelso's nose was flared and the corners of his mouth turned down. "Be careful wot you say. You may have to eat your words."

"I don't think you can do it by yourself."

"You'd better think again."

Dunbar gave a half-smile. "If your memory works at all, you'll recall that you ended up on the floor the first time."

"Because you hit me when I wasn't looking."

"Oh, come on, now. You know you were trying to get in the first punch."

Kelso drew himself up to his full height, and his face grew long. "Are you calling me a liar? Your memory must not be any good, or you'd remember the last fella who tried to talk to me that way."

"Of course I remember. All you did was talk. You let your friend do the shooting. But he's not here now."

I had been wondering where Holcomb was and why Kelso was making a move by himself. I imagined he had decided on short order, knowing that the deputy was gone, and he must have thought he could do better against Dunbar with a gun than with his fists.

Dunbar spoke again. "And in answer to your question, yes, I'm calling you a liar."

Kelso's eyes shifted. I thought he was going queasy, but he pulled himself together. He tipped his head to one side and said, "I've known your type before." With his left hand he took off his hat and swept it downward in front of him. When the hat went below his waist, his .45 came into view.

Dunbar was ready and fired two times.

Kelso lurched, bent forward, dropped his ivory-handled pistol, and fell to the ground.

Dunbar kept his gun pointed as he said, "And I've known your type as well."

He looked at me, and I realized I had my own gun drawn.

"I'm glad you didn't have to use that," he said.

"I think I could have."

"What I meant was, I'm glad things didn't go in such a way that you would have to."

There was not a particle of bragging in the way he said it. To the contrary, it was the first time I had seen a hint of Dunbar recognizing that someone else could get the best of him.

CHAPTER FOURTEEN

A dog was barking, and voices carried from the main street a couple of blocks away. From the intonation, it sounded as if men were calling across the street to one another to ask about the shots they had just heard. Dunbar had holstered his gun and was surveying the area around us.

"I wonder where Holcomb is," he said.

"I don't know." As soon as I said it, I felt foolish, as if there were some way I might have known. But my words meant nothing, and they were gone in a second.

Kelso's dead body, on the other hand, lay in plain view where he had died in the street. I expected someone to come hurrying from downtown—a storekeeper pressing a hat onto his head, or the barber still carrying his razor. But nobody showed.

Dunbar spoke. "I think I'd better go tell Rutledge about this. I don't think there's more than one version to this story, but as a rule, it's good to get yours in first."

"Shall I go with you?"

"Maybe you should stay here—no, it would be better if you didn't. We don't know where Holcomb is."

"Should I wait somewhere?"

"No matter where you go, people are going to ply you with questions. You can come with me if you'd like."

The two of us walked back to the center of town. As soon as we turned the corner onto the main street, I saw men in a half-dozen doorways. They all turned to look at us.

Dunbar said, "Look straight ahead, and keep your wits about you. If Holcomb shows up, these jaybirds won't all be looking at us. So keep an eye out for that."

We walked the two blocks west, nodding at the general store owner, the butcher, and the druggist as we passed them. From across the street, the barber, the postmaster, and the stable man all watched us.

We reached the corner of the Waverly Hotel lot, and I was thinking about how we would walk up the steps onto the shadowed porch, when a voice behind us called out.

"Dunbar!"

We both wheeled around to face Gilbert Rutledge, who seemed to have appeared out of nowhere. After a second of reflection, I figured he had been keeping watch from the side exit of the hotel.

"What the hell's going on?" he said. "Has there been some kind of shooting?"

Dunbar leaned his head to shade out the midday sun with his hat brim. "Yes, there has been. We were looking at Lennox's burned-down house, and Paul Kelso came up behind us. I don't know what his plan was, but he pulled a gun on me. Since we're here and he isn't, you can imagine how it went."

"Is he dead?"

"Yes, he is. Like I said, I don't know if he had a plan. It seemed to me that he decided to take me on while he had the chance. I don't know what he was going to do with Whit or if he even thought that far."

"What a fool. Do you think he was trying to get even for that fight you had before?"

Dunbar looked straight at Rutledge and said, "I think someone has got something he doesn't want anyone to know. That's what all this trouble has been about."

A look of recognition passed over Rutledge's face. "You mean

Rich. He took Agnes and the girls to Glenwood Springs, you know. Or at least to the train."

"I heard he left town." When Rutledge didn't say anything, Dunbar added, "I understand the deputy is out of town as well."

"He went out to Brumley's. He should be back a little later."

"He'll have work waiting for him. Meanwhile, Kelso's lying there where we left him."

"I'll have Mike pick him up. He's the barber, you know."

"I've seen him."

"Meanwhile, I think it would be best if you didn't leave town."

"I wasn't planning to," said Dunbar. "I've got things to tend to."

What things they were, Dunbar did not say. But I surmised that he was expecting someone from the east. We spent the early part of the afternoon in the shade of the small building that served as a stage station. It sat on the eastern edge of town, across from the coal and drayage company, which was closed at the present. I thought we were in for a long wait, as the stage came to town on Tuesdays and Fridays, and today was only Wednesday.

We had been waiting for almost two hours when a speck appeared in the distance. I glanced in that direction every minute or so, and after a while I saw that it was an open wagon drawn by a pair of horses. Two men sat on the seat, and the heads of a couple of other men were visible where they sat in the wagon box.

Dunbar stood up and waited. I rose and stood next to him.

"Friends of yours?" I asked.

"You'll be pleased."

Within a couple of minutes, I smiled. The driver of the wagon was none other than Pat Hendy, filling his half of the seat and swaying with the motion of the wagon. He wore his usual brown hat with a domed crown, and his straight hair stuck out beneath it. His full face had broadened in a smile, and he raised his hand to wave at us.

As the wagon rolled to a stop in a thin cloud of dust, I took a look at Hendy's three passengers. They were swarthy men, dark-eyed and dark-stubbled, dressed in laboring clothes. Two of them wore short-brimmed, flat-crowned hats, and the third one wore a red-and-yellow handkerchief tied over his head.

As the men climbed down from the wagon and brushed off the road dust, Dunbar looked them over. He turned to Hendy with a cheerful expression, and as they shook hands, he said, "It looks like you've got some good helpers here."

"You bet. Took me an extra day to get 'em together, but they're good. Bohemians, from Nebraska. They've worked for me before, them and others. You said in your wire that you had a small job, so I brought a skeleton crew." Hendy laughed. "I'm sure we can knock it out."

I followed Dunbar's gaze to the wagon box. In the front part, there was an assortment of valises and canvas duffel bags, which the men had been sitting and leaning on. Farther back, I saw a supply of picks, shovels, and two wheelbarrows.

Dunbar said, "You've got the right equipment as well."

"Ha-ha. This'll give us the chance to show these folks what we can do." Hendy's eyes roved over Dunbar. "You didn't say where the job was, but I know you need to keep a telegram short."

"It's here in town."

"Oh, that's good. We can get started this afternoon if you want." Hendy raised his voice. "Hey, boys. Shake it off, and let's go."

The Bohemians had gone around to the back of the building to make water. As we waited, I took a quick glance at Dunbar. He had a plan, all right, and I could understand why he had been willing to send a telegram for Mr. Rutledge a few days earlier.

The workmen came back toward the wagon, buttoning their pants. Hendy said, "Tony, you ride in back with Peter and Henry. Mr. Dunbar can ride up front with me." He turned to me. "Sonny, you can ride in back with my men."

Two minutes later, we were rolling down the main street of Dry Camp. Hendy was so cheerful, and the Bohemians were so curious as they gazed back at the townspeople, that I felt as if there was something almost comic in our passing, as if we were part of a circus parade. But I had an inkling of where we were headed, and I didn't think we would find anything funny there.

Dunbar told Hendy to pull over and stop when we passed the town well. The wagon settled, and the horses snuffled.

"Here?" said Hendy.

"That's right," said Dunbar. "We need to dig up that terrace."

Hendy frowned. "I was told we weren't going to do this job. Did something change?"

"It's a different job."

"Well, I don't know if I should talk to Mrs. Stanton first. Or her husband. He's the one that has the final say."

"Mrs. Stanton is on vacation with the girls. Mr. Stanton might be back at some point, but I don't think he'll have much to say that will keep us from our purpose."

Hendy's eyes went back and forth. "I don't know, Mr. Dunbar. I'm not sure about goin' onto someone's property with a crew of men and diggin' it up, especially when the owner told me he didn't want to."

Dunbar shrugged. "We can wait for the deputy to get back to town. If you want, you can let your men wash up at the well, and we can unload some of the equipment."

Hendy drummed his fingers on his knee. "We can do the first

part." Turning in his seat, he said, "Boys, we can wash up here."

The one called Tony stood up in the bed of the wagon and said, "Then the job, huh?"

"Yeah, but we're not gonna get started quite yet."

The men climbed down from the wagon and pumped water for one another as they washed their faces and drank from cupped hands. The rest of us climbed down as well. I stood at the back of the wagon and watched.

Three separate men approached from town, some forty yards apart from one another, all of them rather tentative but not stopping. The Bohemians laughed at some joke between them, then left the well and strolled over to the base of the terrace. Hendy and Dunbar were exchanging a few words in a low voice.

The atmosphere changed when the back door of the house opened and a person walked out through the dusty wisteria vines. As he turned and faced us, I recognized the loose carriage and forward-leaning posture of Holcomb the Hawk. He had his hand poised over his yellow-handled revolver as he looked down at our group. He bored in on us with his hawk nose and his narrow, puffy eyes.

He said, "I don't know what you think you're doin' here, but you-all had better get the hell out."

"Where's your boss?" asked Dunbar.

"Don't worry about him. He told me to keep an eye on things, and that's what I'm doin'."

"You should have kept an eye on your friend Kelso. He came out on the short end."

"I can't help that."

"Not now. But you're on the wrong side of things. You could change that, but you'd rather take orders from your boss."

Movement at the edge of my vision caused me to turn. The three men from town had stopped together at the well and were paying close attention.

Holcomb's eyes flickered to the men and came back. "Don't worry about who I take orders from."

Dunbar spoke in a loud, steady voice. "It's a losing cause, and you're standing on the evidence."

Holcomb frowned. "You don't make any sense, mister. But I do. I'm tellin' you plain and simple to pack up your foreigners and get out."

"And if I don't, are you going to shoot me?"

Holcomb made a small motion with his gun hand. "Don't push me and find out."

Hendy stepped wide of Dunbar. The Bohemians had backed up from the edge of the terrace to the side of the wagon.

Dunbar stood his ground, his own hand ready. "Did your boss tell you to go after me?"

"Oh, shut up."

"Just like he told you to go after Willard and Mrs. Lancaster?"

"I said shut up and get out, or I'll put a bullet through you."

"And the old drunk. But you didn't do that one so well."

Holcomb's body went up and down as he took a breath. He had his elbows pointed outward, and he looked as if he was ready to fly. He put menace in his voice as he said, "I warned you."

Dunbar stayed calm. "Kelso was a fool, and you are, too. Doing another man's dirty work, covering up for something you never had a hand in. You're in so deep, you can't walk away."

"That's it." Holcomb turned and took a step toward the back door, then wheeled and drew. His six-gun roared, and a bullet whined past me.

Dunbar had jumped to the right and had come up with his pistol. He fired once, twice.

Holcomb bent over and tumbled off the edge of the terrace.

The townspeople had scattered, while Hendy and his men had all ducked out of view. I crouched behind the wagon and looked around the side.

Up on the terrace, the door to the house was open. Dunbar kept his eye on it as he held his pistol up and backed out of the line of sight of anyone who might come to the doorway.

Movement and voices in back of me caused me to turn around. Gilbert Rutledge and Deputy Nance were walking toward the well from the direction of the Waverly Hotel. Rutledge spoke to a couple of the townsmen who had moved out of the line of fire, and Nance stood listening with his head forward.

After a moment, Rutledge and Nance approached me where I was crouched by the corner of the wagon. They seemed unconcerned about gunfire, so I stood up.

Rutledge held me with a stern look as he said, "What sense can you give us of this?"

"Well, sir, I think there's a possibility that Mr. Stanton is in the house." I pictured Stanton holed up inside, avoiding Dunbar for one last time, peeking out at the three dark men, and wondering if in some way they had come for him.

Rutledge frowned. "What makes you think so?"

"Holcomb came out of there, and he seemed to be acting on orders."

Rutledge looked at Nance and said, "I thought he was gone, but he may have come back."

Nance's narrow eyes turned to me. "Who shot first?"

"Holcomb did. Half a dozen people saw it."

Nance nodded. I imagined he had already asked the other men. He said, "And you think Stanton's in the house?"

"He could be."

Nance spoke to Rutledge. "I'll go see. But I don't like any of this." With his hand on his revolver handle, he walked across the open ground and climbed up the side of the terrace near the corner of the house. He kept his back against the building, and with his gun drawn, he inched his way to the door. Once there, he spoke in a loud voice.

"Stanton, this is Deputy Nance of the Albany County Sheriff's office. Your man's dead, and we don't need any more trouble. We can talk this over. If you're in there, come out."

A voice sounded from inside, and Nance spoke into the open doorway. I could not hear his words. Then he turned to us and said, "I'm going in. Don't anybody do anything."

All this time, Dunbar had been standing in the shade of the house. Now he crouched and walked to the front corner, then disappeared. A long minute later, he appeared on the other side of the house, at the corner of the terrace.

Another minute passed in silence. I heard the scraping of a chair and an exchange of voices. A few seconds later, Deputy Nance spoke through the open doorway.

"Don't anybody move. Just stay put. We're coming out."

I kept my eye on the doorway. A figure appeared, a blur of tan and brown, and Deputy Nance stepped through the arbor and out into the daylight. Close behind him, Rich Stanton held a gun to his ribs.

"Stand back," said the deputy. He avoided looking at anyone in particular as he moved his head back and forth. He had a hangdog expression on his face, and his narrow shoulders slumped.

Rutledge's voice rose on the air. "Rich, what in the hell—"

"Keep out of it."

In that instant, Deputy Nance grimaced and spun around, raising his left elbow to crack Stanton on the jaw. Stanton's cream-colored hat fell away, and his face tightened as he fired his gun. The deputy cried out in pain and fell to the paving stones as Stanton straightened up and looked around.

I was sure he was looking for the best way to run, but he did not have time. Dunbar rushed across the terrace and tackled him. His gun clattered on the stones, and his hands went out to break his fall. He reached for his gun a couple of feet away, only to have Dunbar's hand come chopping down on his forearm. He raised up on his other side, hooked Dunbar's arm, and rolled with him. Dunbar's hat was gone. Stanton smashed his fist into Dunbar's face, then grabbed his hair and hit him again. Dunbar flailed but could not get loose. Stanton shifted, got a grip on Dunbar's shirt, twisted it, and resumed hammering Dunbar in the face. Dunbar gave a tremendous surge and pushed Stanton halfway off, but they did not separate. Stanton settled into a headlock, then converted it to a choke hold. I could see that he had no desire to get free. To the contrary, he wanted to finish off his nemesis, to keep him from saying another word. He shifted from clamping his forearm against Dunbar's throat to settling both hands on his windpipe and pressing down with all his weight.

I thought, *He's done this before. He knows how to do it.*

Dunbar was making choking, gasping sounds as he struck at Stanton's temple, but the man on top kept his head tucked down.

Dunbar heaved and bucked, then pushed himself up onto one elbow and threw Stanton off balance. As he did, he reached across and pulled Stanton's left hand off his throat.

Stanton grabbed at Dunbar's chin and tried to pull himself on top again, but he had lost his position. He took hold of Dunbar's hair and got him into a headlock again. Then he released the dark hair and slipped his hand down to press against Dunbar's cheek. I did not understand his purpose until I saw his thumb push up into Dunbar's eye.

A sickening jolt hit me in the pit of my stomach as Dunbar let out an unearthly scream and exploded into fury. With a savage sweep of his hand, he broke Stanton's hold on him and took the upper position. He smashed his fist a half-dozen times into Stanton's face, then grabbed the man by the collar and

John D. Nesbitt

slammed his head onto the flat stone four, five, six, seven times until the man went limp.

Nobody could have stopped Dunbar without a weapon, and now the struggle was over. Stanton had wanted to take it to the end, but he did not do things well enough and had brought the end upon himself. He lay motionless as Dunbar crawled off to the side and took in huge, heaving breaths.

During this same time, the deputy had rolled over onto his stomach and was pulling himself across the terrace by his elbows. With his back to the fight, now over, he settled his hand onto the six-gun Stanton had dropped.

"I don't think you'll need that," said Rutledge. "But we'd better see how bad you're shot."

The deputy's face was drained of color. He said, "I need a drink of water."

"We'll get you one." Rutledge turned around to the onlookers from town, who had grown in number to half a dozen. "For God's sake, one of you go in the house and get a cup."

Hendy spoke up. "We've got some tin cups in the wagon. You, Henry, get us some cups."

The Bohemian with the red-and-yellow handkerchief on his head jumped up into the wagon and rummaged among the gear. He came up with two tin cups and handed them to his boss.

Rutledge spoke to the townspeople again. "One of you go for Mike. Tell him to bring bandages. This man's hurt." He took a cup from Hendy and said, "Another one of you, fill this with water for the deputy."

Hendy held a cup toward me. "Here, get some water for Dunbar."

By the time I had a cup of water, Dunbar had found his hat and put it on. With slow, careful steps he came down from the terrace and took the cup.

210

"Thanks." He tipped the cup for several seconds until he drank all the water.

"More?" I asked.

"In a minute."

I studied his face. His right eye was bloodshot, his forehead was scraped, and he had nicks on both cheekbones. A smudge of dust stuck to his left ear. "Are you all right?" I asked.

"I think so."

Rutledge took a second cup of water from the onlookers and handed it to the deputy, who had pulled himself around and was sitting against the outside of the house. "We've got someone coming," Rutledge said. He took a deep breath and squared his shoulders. "And now, Mr. Dunbar, we need an explanation."

Dunbar's eyes were half-closed, and he looked exhausted. "I think you might have some of it figured out," he said.

"Only what you said before. That someone had something serious to hide."

Dunbar motioned with his head toward the terrace. "Your son-in-law, of course. He knew he was at his last ditch. If he could have me killed, or, in the end, do it himself, he might have been able to lie himself out of the worst part."

"And that is—?"

Dunbar held his eyes on Rutledge. "I have good reason to believe he has Louise Brumley buried beneath this terrace."

Rutledge looked as if someone had kicked him in the stomach. "Where in the hell do you get that idea?"

Dunbar blinked as he took a slow breath. "It all adds up. Louise Brumley disappeared at the time your son-in-law was building this house. When his wife wanted to have some excavation done, he shut down one bid after another."

Rutledge's eyes moved side to side as he studied Dunbar and glanced at the dead body of his son-in-law. "That's pretty slim evidence. And you were going to hire these men to dig up this terrace?"

"I still am, and I think we'll find the remains of a woman in a lavender dress."

"There's got to be more to it than this."

"Oh, there is. It goes back a long ways. Rich Stanton was courting your daughter. Louise Brumley was restless in her marriage. Ross Guilford told Jack Brumley he could tell him something but he wouldn't. Everyone thought Louise ran off with a stranger, and time went on. Willard learned from his father that Ross Guilford knew something, but Willard never knew anything more than his father did. Ross never peeped. But Stanton thought he did, so he had Ross done away with. Then Willard. Then Jane Lancaster was killed after she talked to me. Anyone who knew something or seemed to know something ended up on a list. Ambrose Lennox, and then me."

Rutledge narrowed his eyes. "What did that old bitch Jane Lancaster have to say?"

Dunbar took in a breath as he seemed still to be getting his strength back. "Something interesting. She said she thought Louise might have been with child—expectant, to use her word—by a man other than her husband."

"That's no surprise. But you jumped to the conclusion that the man was Rich Stanton? Not that I don't think he was capable, you understand."

"I didn't jump to a conclusion. I had a hunch. And it got stronger when I learned that the man who reported seeing her in North Platte with another man was none other than Rich Stanton. Based on that, I thought there was a good chance that no one ever saw her in another place and that she may well have never left this town."

"And so you reasoned that—"

"She had been here all this time. And it wasn't just an accident that someone wanted to cover up."

"Not a crime of passion."

Dunbar opened his eyes and moistened his lips. "Not in the sense of someone losing his temper all in a moment and not being able to control himself."

Rutledge seemed to be resisting Dunbar's line of thinking. "Why would he have done it, then?"

"Think about it," said Dunbar. "He had a great deal to lose. He had property and money, and he was about to enter into a prestigious marriage. He faced the danger of being exposed."

"Men have been embarrassed by these things before. They don't kill a woman for it, or not usually."

"I think he might have. He faced the prospect not only of having it known that he had an affair with another man's wife, but of having it known that he had mingled with a woman of mixed blood and that he stood to be the father of a child who was not all white. He did not want that knowledge made public, and he did not want that claim on him."

Rutledge's nostrils widened as an expression of disgust passed over his face. "I don't know how much of this I can go along with."

Dunbar shrugged. "I've already arranged to pay for the work. These men are willing to do it, or at least they were when they came here, and the rest of us can stand back and not interfere. Jack Brumley said he thought his wife was wearing a lavender dress and gold earrings when she left. If these men dig up the remains of a woman and even a shred of a lavender dress, you might be convinced that Louise died that same night. Rich Stanton had it planned out when he arranged to meet her."

Rutledge turned his attention to Deputy Nance. The lawman looked forlorn with his pallid face, tired eyes, and slumping shoulders, but he had taken in the whole story.

Rutledge said, "What do you think, deputy?"

Nance pulled in a breath and said, "I got shot in the ribs because people take things into their own hands. First Dunbar and then Stanton, and I don't like it." The deputy rolled a glance toward Stanton's body. "I think the son of a bitch got what was coming to him even if he never touched the Brumley woman. But it sure sounds like he had something to hide, and I'd like to know how much."

Chapter Fifteen

Mike the barber directed a couple of townsmen to cart away the bodies while he tended to Deputy Nance. He cleaned the wound and wrapped a bandage around the man's midsection, then brought out a couple of cushions from the house and arranged a more comfortable seat for the deputy.

Rutledge arched his eyebrows at the sight of the bloodstained man settling himself onto the light tan cushions, but he said nothing.

Meanwhile, the workmen began to take up the paving stones from the terrace. The pick made a crunching sound as Henry swung it to pry up the sandstone slabs. His fellow workers carried the stones off to the side and stacked them. When all but the edges had been stripped away, Hendy gave the order to start digging.

"We might as well start in the middle," he said, his voice still cheerful. "If I had buried someone, that's where I would have put 'em."

The Bohemians took turns, two of them working with the pick and shovel and one of them wheeling the dirt to the far edge of the terrace and dumping it. They had a good audience by now. In addition to the original company of Dunbar, Hendy, Rutledge, Deputy Nance, Mike the barber, and myself, about a dozen men from town, including Ambrose Lennox and a couple of range riders from the Dakota Rose, had joined to form a crowd.

The three men worked on. At first they reminded me of grave-diggers, but as they labored without comment and made the hole wider and deeper, and as I recalled how I thought Stanton might have seen them, I fancied that they were minions of destiny, toiling toward the inevitable.

The moment came. One of the men in the hole spoke to the other in their native language, and he scraped with the shovel. The second man stood aside and watched as Hendy walked to the edge of the hole and looked down. Then the man who had been doing the scraping and digging, the one named Peter, raised the tip of the shovel out of the hole. Entwined with large crumbs of hard dirt was a swatch of lavender cloth.

Hushed comments ran through the crowd.

Rutledge had been standing near where the deputy sat. Now he took a couple of steps toward the hole and said, "By God, he did do it. The son of a bitch. Practically on the eve of his wedding."

Dunbar and Hendy were standing near the edge of the excavation, following every move. Hendy patted Dunbar on the shoulder and said, "You're a game fellow, my friend. There was a moment when I thought he might get the best of you. What would have happened then? Had you told anyone else about your hunch?"

"No, I hadn't. That was a mistake. But he made one, too."

"When he tried to gouge your eye instead of keeping on trying to choke you?"

"Well, that. But his bigger mistake was that even up to the end, he thought he could get away with it."

When the last of the remains were brought up out of the hole, Deputy Nance and Mike the barber took over. The deputy gave instructions for the barber and another man to lay the bones, fragments, and scraps of cloth on a sheet of canvas. One gold earring came up as well. As the men were handling the remnants, Deputy Nance told Rutledge that the crowd could leave now.

Hendy insisted that Dunbar and I join him and his men for a round of drinks, so the six of us went to the Dakota Rose. An exhaustion seemed to have settled upon Dunbar, so we had only one drink and checked back into Hunton's lodging house.

In the seclusion of our room, I felt I could say things I had been keeping to myself. I began by saying, "It's hard to believe someone can do what Stanton did, but I don't suppose you're very surprised. You've seen a great deal."

"I have. But it's a new study every time. It's bad enough that he's ashamed of a woman that another man was proud of, and that he could have her for his pleasure and then do away with her when the danger got too high—that in itself shows amazing selfishness. But then a person wonders, why did he want her? Just for pleasure? Probably not. He wanted to cross the line and mingle with the dark element, as I said earlier. He wanted to take possession, and he wanted to indulge in what was forbidden, at least by his standards. At the same time, one can't help thinking there was something in the indulgence that he loathed—something in himself that he hated and wanted to hide at all costs."

"And the idea that once he did it, he thought he should get away with it. As if he thought he deserved it. I think that causes me to despise him as much as anything. At least there's an end to him."

Dunbar raised his heavy eyelids. "Yes, but there's a thousand more just like him out there somewhere."

Dunbar showed no impatience as we sat through Hunton's breakfast, but I could tell he was ready to go. Leaving Hunton's, we lost no time fetching our horses at the stable and riding out to Carlyle's.

Once we were there, he said, "Whit, this is where the old cowpuncher hits the trail."

I spoke the obvious. "You're leaving?"

"It's time. There's nothing more for me to do here."

I recoiled. "What about Medora? Are you just going to leave her?"

"Not 'just,' but yes."

"Why?"

His dark eyes studied me, as if he was deciding how much he could say that I would understand. "I have more things to do."

I was about to tell him I thought he was a fool when he gave a light smile. "But there's nothing in the larger rules of the universe, or even in what someone could call fate or destiny, that would determine that I couldn't see her again."

He did not fail me. He went from the plain style of the old cowpuncher to the celestial style and back to the old pal.

"Were you afraid I was going to leave her to defend herself against the likes of Pat Hendy?"

"I hadn't thought of that yet, but it would have been a cause for worry."

"She can take care of herself in that way, I assure you."

"I believe it." After a second I added, "Are you going back through town, then?"

"I had that in mind."

"Would you object to my riding that far with you?"

"But no further. If you don't stay around for Eva—well, I couldn't let you leave, that's all. Even if I have to nail your shoes to the floor."

In spite of a few scrapes and bruises, Dunbar had shaved and put on a clean shirt, and he looked well restored as we set out. He rode the blue roan and led the buckskin packhorse. I heard him whistling "Red River Valley" when he got out half a length ahead of me, and when we tied up in front of the Deville Café, he had a spring in his step.

I did not know what kind of a tone to expect when we walked into the café and found Jack Brumley seated at a table across from Medora.

"Come and sit here," he said.

Medora rose from her chair and signaled for us to sit down. When we did, she remained standing. I stole a look at her. With her dark, wavy hair, richly textured skin, and full figure, she was quite a woman for someone to be leaving behind.

Jack did not pay any special attention to her. He turned his tired eyes toward Dunbar and said, "I need to thank you for what you did. For as much as it hurts to learn the truth, it's good to know what actually happened. At least I know she never ran off on Willard. As for that other part—well, it's hard to take, once the facts are there."

Medora said, "You need to forgive her, Jack. It would be the best thing for both of you."

Jack's eyes misted as he answered her. "I forgave her a long time ago, or at least I forgave her for what I thought she did. But it's as if I have to start over now that I know who she had . . . strayed with. As it turned out, it was what did her in."

Medora's dark eyes softened. "She had her weaknesses, Jack. She was human."

"I know. And I tell myself that whatever she did, there's no need to take it as if it was something she did to me."

Medora put her hand on Jack's shoulder. "She may have had reasons that wouldn't make sense to any of us at this point."

Jack nodded. "I suppose so. I'll remember her as the best way I knew her, a beautiful woman." He shifted in his seat and held out his hand to Dunbar. "Thanks for what you did."

As he said it the second time, I realized he may have been

thanking Dunbar for finishing off Stanton as well as for bringing out the truth.

Dunbar said, "You're welcome." After he withdrew his hand,
he met Medora's eyes and said, "I've got my things packed, and
I thought I'd stop here to say good-bye."

She did not show surprise or disappointment. Rather, I
sensed that they already had an understanding. For all I knew,
Dunbar may have seen her on his early-morning walk as well.
Then, as if they had the most mundane of friendships, she said,
"If you wait outside, I'll get you some biscuits to take on the
trail."

"I'll bring the horses around back. Save you a few steps."

"Of course."

Even that much showed me how well they understood each
other. He had as much as said, "Let's not say good-bye in the
street," and she had shared the sentiment.

I walked out the front door with Dunbar. I could say good-
bye in the street, but when the actual moment came, I had a
lump in my throat. I said, "Thanks for everything you did here."

"Thanks for your help."

We shook hands, and I saw the dark spot in his palm for the
last time. He pulled on his gloves and glanced up at the sky.
"Looks like I can get in a few miles before the day's over."

I thought I had a dozen questions I wanted to ask him, but
none of them mattered enough at this point. I said, "I hope you
have safe travels."

"The same for you, my friend." He held me with his dark
eyes. "The road of life goes one way. We don't get to go back
and redo any of it. I hope yours goes well."

He pulled himself into the saddle with one hand as he held
the lead rope with the other. He rode east to the corner of the
street and turned to go in back of the café.

Moisture welled in my eyes, and I did not want to be seen

that way, so I walked east toward the edge of town. I crossed the street Dunbar had turned on, and I kept walking until I passed the coal and drayage company. Out in the open, I turned and gazed to the north, where the vast rangeland stretched away and the distant mountains rose in the haze. After a couple of minutes, movement caught my eye. A rider with a dark hat was moving away from town at a lope. He rode a blue roan and led a buckskin with canvas packs. I smiled at the thought that he was beginning his long journey back to the land of the pale blue snow.

I had nowhere to go at the moment, and my eyes had dried, so I returned to the café. As a matter of courtesy, I sat down again with Jack Brumley, though I couldn't think of a thing we had in common to talk about. Medora came into the dining room looking quite composed. Her dark eyes were calm, and her face was neither flushed nor pale.

She said, "Would you like a cup of coffee, Whit?"

"I don't know."

"I hope you're not in a hurry to go anywhere."

"Oh, no."

I was afraid silence was going to set in, but the front door opened and the bell jingled. In walked Pat Hendy. He was not quite jaunty, but he was not morose like the last time he left town. Through the window I saw his wagon in the street with his three workmen lounging against the baggage in the back.

He took off his domed hat and said to Medora. "This is a bad habit I have of leaving this town. But I never know when I might come back."

"We're always here," she said.

He hesitated, as if he was planning his approach. "You're not going anywhere, then."

"Oh, I couldn't say. I suppose I meant that the café would be here."

"Ah-hah." He paused, and then with his usual lack of reserve he said, "Are you someone else's girl?"

Her eyebrows went up a little. "I wouldn't go so far as to say that."

"But you won't say that you aren't."

"You could put it that way if you wanted."

He seemed to take heart. "Then you're not."

"No." But she could not suppress a smile as she said, "Not yet."

Pat Hendy did not return to Dry Camp. From time to time I have thought of him, undaunted, moving quantities of dirt with the help of Bohemian, Irish, or Chinese laborers. I sometimes wonder if he has gone on to acquire a dragline or a steam shovel. I imagine he has found a woman to match his mettle—someone bright-eyed, perhaps a bit stout, and tending to speak her mind.

Closer to home, things have followed their courses. The Clay Creek Ranch was taken over by new owners, and I went back to learn the cowhand trade. I helped out Jack Brumley on the side. From time to time I rode past the place where he had Louise's remains buried next to Willard's grave, and one day I helped bury him there.

As my interest in Eva developed and was returned, I had to decide whether I should, like some cowboys did when they got married, quit punching cows, or whether I should, like other punchers, buy a few cows of my own. I chose the latter, and Eva and I settled down on the old Brumley place. We have brought it back to life, and at the same time we have become caretakers of the three graves.

During the time that I was working for wages and courting Eva, Medora sold the café to Eva's parents. I am not sure where she went to, and for all I know, she might be out on the Elsinore Grand. Eva's parents run a good business and expect to hear from her again some day.

Ambrose Lennox lived on a few more years, staying in Jane Lancaster's house. When his time came, he joined Jane and his old friend Ross Guilford in the quiet cemetery at the edge of town.

Gilbert Rutledge, after helping sell the Clay Creek Ranch, moved his daughter and her two perfect daughters to Des Moines. He leased the Waverly Hotel to a man who has now paid it off over a course of ten years. Rutledge gave up on the plan for the town of Madeleine. The last time I rode down that way, the site was still nothing more than dust and grass and sagebrush.

The Stanton house has been up for sale for these ten years, but no one has ever bought it or lived in it. I have not peeked in through the windows, but I have heard that the furniture and the curtains have been much chewed by mice. Out back by the terrace, the wisteria vines have died, the lilac bushes have withered, the paving stones sit where Pat Hendy's workmen left them, and the hole fills in an inch or so each year as the wind moves the dirt.

ABOUT THE AUTHOR

John D. Nesbitt lives in the plains country of Wyoming, where he teaches English and Spanish at Eastern Wyoming College. He writes western, contemporary, mystery, and retro/noir fiction as well as nonfiction and poetry. John has won many awards for his work, including two awards from the Wyoming State Historical Society (for fiction), two awards from Wyoming Writers for encouragement of other writers and service to the organization, two Wyoming Arts Council literary fellowships (one for fiction, one for nonfiction), two Will Rogers Medallion Awards (one for western poetry, one for fiction), and three Spur awards from Western Writers of America. His most recent books are *Dark Prairie* and *Death in Cantera,* frontier mysteries with Five Star.

The employees of Five Star Publishing hope you have enjoyed this book.

Our Five Star novels explore little-known chapters from America's history, stories told from unique perspectives that will entertain a broad range of readers.

Other Five Star books are available at your local library, bookstore, all major book distributors, and directly from Five Star/Gale.

Connect with Five Star Publishing

Visit us on Facebook:
   https://www.facebook.com/FiveStarCengage

Email:
   FiveStar@cengage.com

For information about titles and placing orders:
   (800) 223-1244
   gale.orders@cengage.com

To share your comments, write to us:
   Five Star Publishing
   Attn: Publisher
   10 Water St., Suite 310
   Waterville, ME 04901